SUMMER SECRETS

A LADY GAYLE SUMMER MYSTERY

CASSIE RUSH

Published: August 2023

Gordian Knot Publishing

Paperback ISBN: 978-1-913948-07-8

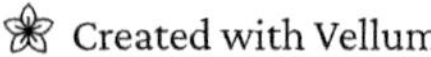

CHAPTER ONE

Lady Gayle Summer gripped the bannister rail and gave into a fit of coughing before she attempted to walk downstairs to her dining room, where breakfast awaited. It had been several days since she'd managed to leave her bedroom, and she was desperate for a change of scenery. She inhaled deeply, but all that did was make the pain and the coughing worse.

'Hang it all,' she said. Before she could make the decision to return to her bedroom, her maid, Alice, was by her side.

'Perhaps another day of rest, milady,' said Alice in a tone that sounded more like she was giving an order than a suggestion.

On the point of protesting, Lady Gayle's body was wracked by more coughing. Her lungs scratched against her rib cage, and she bit back a squeal of anguish. She nodded wordlessly and allowed Alice to guide her back to her bedroom suite.

'I'm going to ask Mr Fredericks to call Dr Sloane,' said Alice. 'I don't like the sound of that cough.'

'You're not the only one,' said Lady Gayle. 'I don't much like the sound of it myself.' Once back in her room, Lady Gayle made for the armchair by the fire. She found that lying down made her cough much worse, even though sitting up did nothing to relieve the pain in her ribs. She rubbed at her rib cage, wishing that the pain could be alleviated. However, she knew, only too well that recovery from influenza would take some time.

Alice rang the bell for the kitchen and placed a request for a hot lemon and honey drink to be brought up to her ladyship. Within moments, it seemed the butler, Fredericks, was delivering the beverage along with a glass of brandy.

'It will help with the pain, my lady,' he said. 'I have telephoned Dr Sloane, and he promises to be here this afternoon. Will there be anything else, my lady?'

Lady Gayle held the glass of hot toddy to her nose and breathed in the steam, hoping that it would ease her chest. Instead, it brought on another bout of coughing, and she leaned forward in her armchair, holding onto her ribs and cursing the influenza.

Alice passed her the glass of brandy; she took two large mouthfuls and swallowed them down quickly.

'I am so glad,' she said, 'that the new fashions mean I'm not wrapped up in corsets.'

Alice dipped her head, trying to hide a smile, 'There's every chance, milady. I think your old corsets were put in the attic. I could fetch some down for you, but of course, it might stop you coughing altogether.'

'Yes, Alice,' said Lady Gayle. 'You could be right. After all, they usually managed to stop me breathing.' She held her breath for a moment, waiting for another bout of coughing to begin. Fortunately, the feeling passed, but beads of sweat were forming on her upper lip. 'I think I've changed my mind though. I would like to go back to bed.'

'Very good, milady,' replied Alice. 'Perhaps if you try to sleep?'

'I think I would prefer to sit up, at least for a while. Charles Vickery has written to me, and I'd quite like to read his letter and write back this afternoon.'

Alice nodded. She helped her mistress to bed, then collected the writing tray and placed it on the bed close to her ladyship. She added a couple of pillows behind Lady Gayle's back to enable her to sit up more easily.

'Will that be all, milady?'

Lady Gayle nodded. 'Yes. Thank you. I'll ring if I need you.'

Alice bobbed a curtsy, and Lady Gayle turned her attention to the letter from Viscount Charles Vickery.

She sliced open the envelope, noticing the Italian stamp with a raise of her eyebrows. 'What on earth is he doing in Italy, I wonder,' she murmured. Placing the letter opener on the tray, she pulled out the letter and settled down to read.

As was typical of Lord Charles, the note was quite short. 'I'm in Tuscany,' he wrote. 'Weather absolutely splendid. Felicity Makepeace is here too. Such a shame you're too ill to make it. I'm sure you would love this little village and the wonderful food.'

Lady Gayle laid the letter on the writing tray, wishing she was well enough to travel. She took another sip of brandy and began to write a reply. However, feeling as if she had no news of her own to report, she allowed the pen to drop from her fingers. With a sigh, she rubbed her forehead and drank the last of the now lukewarm hot toddy.

Exhaustion wafted over her, and she pushed the writing tray to one side, nudged the extra pillows on the floor, and settled down to rest. Although she only planned to rest her eyes for a moment, the next thing she knew was that Alice was bent over her, shaking her awake to say the doctor had arrived.

'There's not really a lot I can do for you,' said Dr Sloane. 'I'll give you some painkillers, but it's really a case of allowing the pleuritic sacks on your lungs to become less swollen.'

'How can I do that, Doctor?' said Lady Gayle.

'You know exactly what I'm going to say, your ladyship,' said the doctor with a smile. 'Bed rest.'

'That's not something I'm very good at, Doctor,' replied Lady Gayle. 'Wouldn't fresh air help me more?'

'Normally, I would say yes,' replied the doctor. 'Spring, however, is very late arriving in Yorkshire this year; the air is still quite cold and damp. It will do your lungs no good at all, unlike a visit to somewhere warm. On the other hand, when you feel up to it, a short stroll in the garden may help. But you must make sure you're well wrapped up.'

'Very good, doctor,' said Lady Gayle. She bade him farewell and asked Alice to prepare one of the painkillers for her. As Alice closed the bedroom door behind her, Lady Gayle picked up the letter from Charles Vickery once more. She had an idea, and she pulled the writing tray close and began her letter.

Two days later, Lady Gayle convinced herself that she was well enough to leave the house. With Alice in attendance, she managed to potter to the stables to visit Plantagenet, the grey horse she had inherited from her late father.

'I do miss our gallops across the fields, old boy,' she said. She hung her head and rested her forehead against the horse's muzzle whilst biting back another bout of coughing.

'That still sounds nasty,' said a voice behind her.

Lady Gayle whirled around and, standing behind her, his arms folded across his chest, was Harry Howden, her land agent. Torn between offering her hand for him to shake and covering her mouth with the same hand, she decided to cover her mouth. 'I'm almost on the mend, Mr Howden,' she said. 'Just can't get rid of this cough. Dr Sloane said that fresh air would help but that the air here is still too cold and damp.'

'Perhaps drier, warmer air would help?' said Mr Howden. He smiled, and the sun caught the golden flecks in his hazel eyes.

Lady Gayle's heart gave a little flutter, which caused yet more coughing. 'I quite agree, so does Dr Sloane,' she said. 'Lord Charles is in Tuscany at the moment, staying at a villa with friends. I wrote a letter a few days ago and have just sent him a wire to ask if I might join him.'

'That sounds like a very good idea,' said Mr Howden. The smile left his face, and the gold flecks stopped twinkling.

Lady Gayle, realising she may have made a mistake by mentioning Lord Charles, tightened her jaw. She gave a small shake of her head and turned around to walk back to Bethencourt Castle.

Once back in her castle, she made her way to the drawing room to take tea with her mother.

'Mama, Dr Sloane has suggested I need some convalescence in warmer climes,' she said. Well, it wasn't a complete lie. The doctor had mentioned warm air would help her cough. 'Viscount Charles Vickery is in Tuscany with friends currently. I have written to ask if I might join them for a few days whilst I rid myself of the rest of this illness.'

'Written? Why write when you can send a wireless message?' said her mother. 'I think a change of scenery would do you the world of good, especially after the last few months.'

Lady Gayle gazed at her mother with her head tilted to one side. 'You wouldn't happen to have an ulterior motive, Mama?' she said.

'Why, of course not,' replied her mother. 'I simply happen to be in agreement with you.'

Lady Gayle narrowed her eyes. 'Yes, Mama,' she said. 'I think it's that which disturbs me most.'

CHAPTER TWO

The following morning, Lady Gayle received a telegram from Lord Charles inviting her to come and stay at Villa Montagna Verde. Earl and Countess Harding are dying to meet you. Stop. Come at once. Stop. Felicity thrilled. Stop. Charles. Stop.

Lady Gayle smiled to herself wondering precisely how thrilled the Honourable Felicity Makepeace would be at her presence. It was only a few months ago that Miss Makepeace had been furious at Charles' engagement to Lady Sylvia Redmond-Smythe. Although she'd discovered that Miss Makepeace had been completely innocent of Lady Sylvia's murder, Lady Gayle had long been suspicious of her. She only removed Miss Makepeace from her list of suspects when she uncovered the identity of the real killer. Even the fact that the young woman had reportedly been on her way to the south of France at the time of the murder had not excluded her from the list of suspects. Miss Makepeace was, after all, a skilled racing driver with a high-powered Bugatti at her disposal. She could have easily committed the murder and made a rapid escape.

Travel arrangements were soon made; Alice packed for warmer weather and two days later, lady and maid were on the train heading towards Dover. Once there, they would make the short crossing over the English Channel. From Calais, they were to take another train to Paris, where they would embark on the Orient Express. The Pullman sleeper would take them to Venice, and from there, another train would transport them to Florence.

The cross-channel ferry was a huge improvement on the troopship Lady Gayle had last travelled to France on in 1916. Even Calais was much cleaner than it had been when she'd last been on this side of the English Channel.

Eyes misting with tears caused by too many memories, Lady Gayle boarded the train to Paris, grateful that they were going nowhere near Amines, where she had served as an ambulance driver on the Western Front. She opened the novel that she had brought with her. After having read the opening paragraph at least five times, she gave up. She knew the reason she was unable to concentrate on the words was entirely due to her mixed feelings at being back in France.

She closed her eyes and then snapped them open again —eyes wide and heart pounding. *I can't remember his face.* Scrabbling in her handbag, she brought out the small photograph she had placed safely in a side pocket just before departing. She sat tracing the line of his jaw with her fingertip.

Still handsome in his Royal Warwickshire regimental uniform, Lieutenant Hugh Sexton smiled back at her. She sniffed and dabbed delicately at her nose before sitting up, spine straight and her shoulders back. With one last glance at her late husband's face, she replaced the photograph in her handbag and turned her attention to the passing landscape. Fields gave way to a more industrial view as they drew closer to Paris.

Changing trains to the Pullman Orient Express was easy enough, and soon, Lady Gayle was ensconced in her sleeper compartment with Alice.

'I don't feel right being here in first class,' said Alice, looking at the bunks which would form their beds for the night.

'Stuff and nonsense,' said Lady Gayle. 'I couldn't have you sitting up all night while I was here in comfort. It wouldn't feel right. I know people who do that to their staff, but I don't want to be one of those people.'

'I'm ever so grateful, milady, but that guard gave me a funny look. I could have sworn he was going to throw me off.'

Lady Gayle shrugged. 'I do believe that's why he paid such attention to the tickets. But never mind. We're here now, and we can enjoy ourselves.'

'It is lovely to be heading towards nicer weather,' said Alice. She glanced towards the window, which gave out onto the corridor and squealed. Two men in black shirts, their hands cupped around their eyes, were staring through the glass.

'Don't worry, Alice. They have no jurisdiction here. They don't have any in Italy either, but that doesn't seem to stop them.' Lady Gayle sighed. Benito Mussolini's black-shirted militia were increasing in number and ferocity. After their march on Rome the previous autumn, Mussolini had taken on the role of Italian Prime Minister. Lady Gayle fervently hoped they would not encounter any of the fascist militia while they were in Tuscany.

She turned to her travel guide. 'Perhaps we should focus on nicer things, Alice,' she said. 'We can visit several vineyards in the region. There are a number of different grape varieties grown too.'

'It would be nice to see grapes growing, milady,' said Alice. 'I wouldn't be able to drink any wine though. I would get terribly tipsy.'

'Don't worry, Alice,' said Lady Gayle. 'I'm sure I could manage to drink your wine for you.'

Alice tittered into her hand and flashed a smile at her ladyship.

Lady Gayle bit back her chuckle. Although improving, the cough still grated a little. She picked up her novel and flicked through a few pages. Still unable to concentrate on the words, she replaced the bookmark and laid the book beside her. Instead, she gazed out the window and watched the French countryside race by. The green fields, full of crops and animals, were a pleasant change from her last recollections of being in France. She shook her head in an attempt to rid herself of those memories. The rhythm of the train on the tracks was very soothing, and before long, Lady Gayle drifted into sleep.

Alice woke her at teatime, and they made their way to the dining car for afternoon tea.

Once seated and having placed their order, Lady Gayle wasted no time in running an eye over her fellow travellers.

For the most part, she found it easy to work out who people were. The young man with long hair tied into a ponytail had to be an artist or writer. Watching him wave his hands around as he spoke, Lady Gayle noticed his fingernails had paint embedded in the nail bed. Artist, she thought. His companion, however, was harder to assess. A quiet, prim-looking young woman sat opposite him. She scarcely uttered a word, although it would have been difficult to interrupt the flow of his conversation.

What on earth brought those two together, she wondered.

Halfway down the carriage, with grey hair piled high on her head, was a richly dressed woman. Opposite her, dressed in black, was a younger woman who was clearly a maid or a companion. Lady Gayle squinted at the old woman, trying to recollect who she was, and then it came to her. The lady in question was a minor member of a European Royal house. Which house, of course, she couldn't remember, but she had the distinct feeling she'd met the woman before.

'More tea, milady?' Alice had leaned forward and raised the pot over Lady Gayle's teacup.

'Yes, please, Alice,' said Lady Gayle. 'I was just looking at our fellow guests. Quite a rum lot, aren't they?'

Alice dipped her head, but Lady Gayle spotted the grin which had spread across her maid's face.

'So long as there are no murderers amongst them, milady,' said Alice. 'What you need is a nice, quiet break. No excitement. No murderers. And no investigations.'

'That doesn't sound terribly exciting, Alice,' said Lady Gayle. 'Although you are right, it would be nice to have a holiday with no dead bodies.'

'Exactly so, milady.' Alice refreshed her own tea and sat back, sipping delicately with her small finger raised. When she replaced her teacup on the table, she nibbled at a sandwich, and she too began to take a look around the carriage at her fellow travellers.

Lady Gayle watched her maid people-watching, smiling to herself until Alice's eyes rested on one person and did not look away. Lady Gayle half-turned to see who it was who had caught Alice's attention.

Sitting on his own and partially hidden behind a newspaper was a man around thirty years of age, dressed in a suit.

Lady Gayle turned her attention to Alice and said, 'What is it about him that's piqued your curiosity?'

'He doesn't fit in, milady,' whispered Alice. 'It's a nice suit, but it's not tailored.'

'What difference does that make?' said Lady Gayle.

'It means, milady, that he's not a gentleman. And if he's not a gentleman, what's he doing in first class?'

'I didn't realise you were such a snob, Alice,' replied Lady Gayle with a giggle.

'I don't think I am, milady.' Alice looked rather miffed at the idea. 'It's just that he doesn't fit in. Everyone else comes from money. Even the artist at the end there looks very scruffy, but you can see he's using his old-school tie as a belt. And, if I'm not very much mistaken, it's an Etonian tie.'

'My word, Alice,' breathed Lady Gayle, 'you've become very good at this.'

'Mr Sherlock Holmes,' said Alice, as if that explained everything, which, of course, it did. 'One of the young men I tended to in Wimeraux was very keen on the work of Mr Conan Doyle, and I used to read it to him.' Alice's eyes glittered, and she glanced out of the window for a moment.

Lady Gayle didn't interrupt. All too often, she found her own thoughts drifting back to times during the Great War, hard as she tried to put those memories behind her. She snatched another look at the man in the grey suit. As she did, he folded his newspaper, rose, and placed the paper under his arm. Before he was able to button up his jacket, Lady Gayle caught a glimpse of the hidden holstered pistol.

Glancing at her maid, she saw that Alice had spotted it too.

CHAPTER THREE

THE REMAINDER OF THE JOURNEY PASSED UNEVENTFULLY, THE MAN with the gun wasn't seen at dinner nor at breakfast the following morning. At first, Lady Gayle wondered where he had got to, but by the time the train pulled into Venice, she had already put him out of her mind. Alice found a porter to take their luggage to the connecting train.

'Alice,' said Lady Gayle, 'I'm going to find out how long we have to wait for our train. Will you stay here and take care of the luggage?'

'Yes, milady,' replied Alice, who was already regarding the station porter with a baleful eye. 'I'll meet you on the platform.'

Lady Gayle watched as Alice, unable to speak Italian, showed the porter the train and destination she had written down. The porter set off at a rapid pace, and Alice scurried along behind him. *Well, let's hope I see them again.* She saw a sign that read *Informazioni di Viaggio* and hoped her rudimentary Italian would get her the information she required.

With a duplicate of the information she'd given to Alice,

she passed the slip of paper with Firenze written on it to the clerk in the information kiosk. To check that she had understood, she wrote down the time and the platform number on the slip of paper and showed it to the clerk, who nodded rapidly.

I must learn some more Italian, she thought as she wandered away. She glanced at her watch and checked it against the station clock. They had a two-hour wait until their train left. If she could locate Alice easily and find somewhere to leave the luggage, they could perhaps enjoy a light meal by the side of the canal before the next part of their journey.

Lady Gayle made her way to the platform, showing her tickets to a guard. Alice and the porter stood side-by-side, Alice with her arms folded.

'I thought we could get a little bite to eat, Alice,' said Lady Gayle. 'I'm sure we can find a café quite easily.'

'What about the luggage, milady?' said Alice. 'We can't leave it here.'

'Perhaps the porter would stay with the suitcases?' said Lady Gayle.

'I wouldn't know how to ask him, milady. Would you?' replied Alice.

'May I be of assistance?'

Lady Gayle turned to face the newcomer. It was the grey-suited man from the train. From his accent, she judged him to be an American. Alice had been right; it was exactly why he'd looked out of place—a different style of tailoring. He stood in front of her, his hat raised in a chivalrous manner. With an amused gleam in his chocolate brown eyes, he was clearly awaiting a response. The gun and holster were no longer in evidence. However, a badge was clipped to his belt. Lady Gayle recognised it as belonging to the Pinkerton Detective Agency.

'We have a two-hour wait before our train leaves,' said Lady Gayle. 'Unfortunately, my Italian is not good enough to ask the porter if he can stay with the luggage.'

'It's unlikely he would do that in any case, ma'am,' said the newcomer. He turned to the porter and issued a few orders in rapid Italian.

The porter nodded and placed the luggage against the railed fence. The stranger spoke to the train guard, who issued a ticket, and stood waiting with his hand out.

'He wants paying, ma'am. You'll find somebody else to put your luggage on the train when it arrives.'

Lady Gayle opened her small bag to retrieve her purse. She paid the guard, who handed her the small ticket. 'I can't thank you enough, Mr...?' she said.

'Alex Cornwall, at your service,' he said, tipping his hat.

'Oh, you're American,' said Lady Gayle, as if she'd just noticed his accent. 'What brings you to Venice?'

'Business,' replied Alex Cornwall.

Lady Gayle held her hand out, 'Lady Gayle Summer,' she said. 'My maid, Alice, and I are on holiday.'

'Well, have a lovely time,' he said. 'Give that ticket to the guard when you come back, and he'll make sure that your luggage gets put on the train.' He touched his fingertips to the brim of his trilby and strolled away.

Lady Gayle watched him walk away until, at her side, Alice gave a small cough. 'Shall we take a stroll, milady?'

'Yes, Alice,' said Lady Gayle. 'I'd really like to stretch my legs.'

Outside the Santa Lucia railway station, gondolas bobbed on the canal. Passengers from other trains were standing aside whilst their luggage was loaded onto the waiting gondolas and taken away.

Lady Gayle raised her face to the sun and sighed. ‘I’d forgotten what it felt like to have the sun on your face.’

‘Indeed, milady,’ replied Alice, ‘but we do seem to be rather in the way here. Shall we go and find somewhere to eat?’

Pulled from her reverie, Lady Gayle nodded, cast a look around at her surroundings, and said, ‘Let’s go this way.’ She set off at a brisk pace, and Alice followed along.

Finally settling on a small establishment which had tablecloths on its tiny tables, they sat down, and Lady Gayle ordered for them both. The waiter raised an umbrella to shade them from the sun.

When the food arrived, Alice prodded the risotto with her fork. ‘Is it like kedgeree, milady?’

‘Yes, Alice, it’s exactly like kedgeree, but different,’ replied Lady Gayle.

Alice gave her a quick look with narrowed eyes. ‘I feel like I’ve eaten a lot of kedgeree recently, milady.’ All the same, she picked up a forkful and placed the rice in her mouth with a very doubtful expression on her face. However, her countenance changed to one of bliss as the delicate flavours of the risotto met with her approval.

‘Very nice, milady,’ she said.

Lady Gayle smiled. ‘I thought you’d like it,’ she said.

Lady and maid passed a very relaxed hour together, eating by the canal and soaking up the rays and the sounds of a busy day in Venice.

Sadly, all too soon, it was time to return to the train station and the next part of their journey. Luggage safely stored upon the train, Lady Gayle and Alice found their seats. They were not alone this time, and they continued their journey in silence. Lady Gayle was still unable to lose herself in her new novel, and Alice gazed out at the countryside.

'I'm expecting Lord Charles to meet us at the station, Alice,' said Lady Gayle.

'Will he be with that racing driver?' asked Alice.

'You know, I have absolutely no idea. I would imagine that he will be unless he's been able to rustle himself up a car,' said Lady Gayle, 'but thinking about it, I don't believe Lord Charles likes to drive. So, there's a very good chance it will be Miss Makepeace collecting us.'

'Oh, that will be ever so exciting, milady,' said Alice. 'Do you think she'll drive as quickly as you do?'

'I would imagine, Alice, that she drives even faster than I can. I don't believe I can drive fast enough to race.'

'Oh, I don't know, milady, you do drive ever so fast.'

'I do my best,' said Lady Gayle with a faint smile. *I do wonder what she's like, this racing driver of Charles'. I wonder if she'll make him happy.*

They left the train at Florence, and Alice dashed to the guard's van to ensure that their luggage was safe and that nothing was left behind. With the assistance of another porter, they left the coolness of the station for the warmth of a Tuscan day in early spring.

'Gigi, Gigi.'

Lady Gayle whirled around, shading her eyes with her hand as she searched for the caller. Loitering by the side of an elegant brunette in a peach-tinted, drop-waisted dress stood Charles in a light-coloured linen suit, waving a straw hat in the air.

Returning his wave, Lady Gayle beckoned to Alice and

the porter, and she strode over to Charles and his lady companion.

Lord Charles threw his straw hat in the back of the car and clutched Lady Gayle's upper arms, giving her a peck on both cheeks.

The double kiss, so favoured by the French, brought back memories that she was still fighting to keep in the past. Fixing a smile on her face, Lady Gayle pulled back and said, 'Are you going to introduce me to your companion?'

'Oh, yes. Dash it all. Lady Gayle Summer, allow me to introduce the Honourable Miss Felicity Makepeace.'

CHAPTER FOUR

Lady Gayle held out her hand to find it grasped in a cool but firm grip. For a moment, she wondered if the Honourable Felicity would squeeze her hand in the way that so many military men had done during the Great War —to demonstrate their superior physical power.

She glanced at their clasped hands and then raised her head to look into Felicity Makepeace's dark eyes. There was a hint of infectious amusement lurking in the young woman's face, and Lady Gayle could not help herself but return the smile. As she did so, she reminded herself that as a racing driver, Miss Makepeace would have encountered the same sort of boorish behaviour that she had come across herself. Lady Gayle returned the grin with genuine warmth.

Charles ensured the porter had all the luggage stowed safely, tipped the man, and jumped into the back seat of the Bugatti with a flushed Alice.

Felicity pressed the starter button, and the Bugatti roared into life. Lady Gayle placed her right hand on top of her cloche hat as the car pulled away, leaving her stomach on the station pavement.

Conversation over the roar of the engine and the rushing wind was impossible, but it was not long before they were leaving Florence behind and heading into the hills of Tuscany. The air temperature dropped as the elevation increased, but it was still much warmer than a spring day in North Yorkshire.

They passed through several villages before they passed a sign reading Montecielo. Felicity slowed the car, driving carefully through the village before she turned into the forecourt of a large, pink-painted villa.

'Welcome to the Villa Montagna Verde,' announced Charles. He leapt from the rear seat without waiting for a door to be opened and began to unload the suitcases. 'We've put you in a couple of rooms at the back. Your maid will be in the bedroom next door to yours, Gigi. I hope that's acceptable?'

'It'll be hard cheese if it's not acceptable.'

Lady Gayle turned in the direction of the speaker. Holding a delicate handkerchief to her nose, a woman of middle years strolled towards them. Her blonde hair was cut into a fashionable bob, and she wore very fashionable clothes; a double string of pearls hung straight down over her thin, androgynous figure.

'Ah, Bea,' said Charles. He pointed at Lady Gayle. 'Gigi, this is Bea. The Countess Beatrice Harding. Bea, allow me to introduce Lady Gayle Summer.'

Beatrice Harding nodded but didn't hold out a hand in greeting. Lady Gayle thought it was because she was inserting a cigarette into the end of a long cigarette holder. 'Well, you've rather messed up the numbers.' Bea Harding lowered her sunglasses and regarded the new arrivals. The pupils of her dark eyes were enormous; it was almost impossible to tell the difference between pupil and iris. Hollows underneath her eyes were deep, dark shadows. 'We're an odd number now, but I suppose at least it isn't thirteen.'

'Come along, Bea,' said Charles, 'you said it would be fine. Gigi has been terribly ill and needs the warm weather. She's still got a nasty cough, so you can put that dreadful cigarette away.'

'I don't see that it makes any difference outdoors,' said Bea Harding with a sniff. 'I was just going to sit in the courtyard since it's a little cooler there. It would be absolutely lovely if that blessed fountain were working. I've spoken to the gardener again, but he pretends not to understand my Italian.'

'That's because, my darling, your Italian is absolutely dreadful. He's not pretending he can't understand. He really can't. You must be Lady Gayle.' The new arrival, a florid-looking man, held out his hand and shook Lady Gayle's so hard that it made her wince. 'Richard Harding. Don't listen to my wife. Make yourself at home. We don't stand on ceremony here.' He smiled adoringly at his wife, who returned the expression with a somewhat sarcastic twist to her lips. Earl Harding didn't appear to notice.

Lady Gayle swallowed but gallantly took in the scenery, gazing through the archway to the courtyard where a forlorn-looking fountain hunkered down amongst the weeds. As she returned her gaze to the villa, Felicity Makepeace caught her eye.

'I'm convinced it would work if it weren't ram packed with weeds and dirt,' she said.

'You could be right,' said Lady Gayle. 'Would anyone mind if I took a look at it later?'

Felicity Makepeace shrugged, 'I very much doubt it,' she said. 'In fact, I'm sure Count Bianchi would be delighted. If the fountain worked, he'd be able to charge more for renting out the villa.'

'I see,' said Lady Gayle. 'Charles said he'd been swimming whilst he was here. But I can't see a pool or anything. How far is the sea?'

'Oh, we're too far away from the sea, but if you fancy taking a spin with me, there's a nice lake a little further up into the hills,' said Felicity.

'That would be lovely,' said Lady Gayle. 'When can we go?'

'I thought you were still unwell,' said Felicity. 'Shouldn't we wait until you've recovered a bit?'

'Perhaps, let's see how I feel in the morning.'

Lady Gayle made her excuses and joined Alice upstairs in the suite that had been put aside for them.

'Will you need a lie down, milady?' said Alice.

'No, I don't think I do,' said Lady Gayle. 'I actually feel quite invigorated after that car drive, Miss Makepeace says she'll take me for a swim tomorrow morning.'

'That's very kind of her,' said Alice. 'She seems a very nice young lady. Earl Harding is her uncle, you know. That's why she's staying here.'

Lady Gayle gave Alice a sideways glance. 'How on earth did you find that out?'

'I have my ways, milady,' replied Alice. 'It's always good to keep your ear to the ground.'

'It is indeed Alice. Tell me, has your ear on the ground also told you about her and Charles?'

Alice pursed her lips, 'I'm told the young lady has a new passion now.'

Lady Gayle raised her eyebrows, 'I wonder who that could be?'

'Not a *who*, milady. It's a *what*. The car she was driving,' said Alice. 'Earl Harding's valet, Mr Linden, believes she has eyes for none other than her Bugatti.'

Lady Gayle nodded. It was just as well because she had not sensed any interest in the young lady from Charles. She stepped over to the window, and pushing the lightweight muslin aside, she stared into the courtyard, where Countess Harding sat on one of the stone benches smoking a cigarette. Her husband was nowhere to be seen.

Since there was no cook provided for their stay at the villa, the party made their way into the village of Montecielo and ate dinner at a small restaurant tucked away in the corner of the square.

Looking around the dining area, Lady Gayle ascertained that they were the only non-Italians dining that evening.

'Are we the only English people staying in the village at the moment, Charles?' she said.

'No, no, not at all,' replied Charles. 'Count Bianchi, who owns the villa where we are residing has another one, Villa Colli di Firenze, it's not far from us. He has a group of friends stopping with him.

'Actually, that's him walking in now.' Charles raised his hand in a wave to a handsome grey-haired man wearing a white dinner jacket.

He received a nod of recognition in return as the gentlemen escorted his party to a table on the far side of the dining room.

Lady Gayle gasped as she recognised one of the ladies in the group. Lady Elizabeth Hansen glanced in her direction but gave no indication of recognition or acknowledgement.

'Dash it all,' hissed Lady Gayle to Charles. 'What on earth is she doing here?'

'I have no idea,' replied Charles. 'I thought she and Pongo were staying in Florence. Perhaps they fancied a bit of mountain air now that it's getting warmer?'

'Can you see Pongo? I can't,' said Lady Gayle. 'He doesn't seem to be with the party.'

'No, he's not, is he? I wonder where he's got to.' However, far from looking around for the missing Pongo, Charles took a cigarette from his silver case and tapped the end on the table before lighting it.

'Do you know the others?' said Lady Gayle.

Charles glanced at the recent arrivals. 'Not well,' he said. He looked up at Bea Harding, who had just returned to their table. He briefly rubbed his forefinger under his nose.

The countess repeated the gesture as if it were a secret signal.

Lady Gayle took in her flushed face. She certainly seemed to have more energy and enthusiasm now than she'd had during the afternoon. Her stories about driving a general's staff car during the war were an absolute hoot.

'The tall chap is Teddy Devine,' Charles continued. 'He's American. His father's a banker or something. The other lady is Teddy's cousin, or some close relation or other, I'm not sure which. Julia Fitzpatrick is her name. Rich as Croesus from what I'm told.'

'But not Mr Devine?' asked Lady Gayle, her eyes running over the younger man's impressive physique.

'Fancy him, do you,' said Charles. 'He does have money,

but I think it depends on how well he's getting on with daddy at the time.'

'Of course,' murmured Lady Gayle, briefly thinking of her own father. She'd never have the opportunity to ask him for money ever again.

CHAPTER FIVE

The following morning, Lady Gayle felt much improved after a good night's sleep. Despite the travelling, which had made her tired, the coughing had improved.

'Alice, I think I will go bathing today with Miss Makepeace. Will you lay out my swimming costume for me?' said Lady Gayle.

'If you're sure, milady,' replied Alice. 'Would it not be a better idea to rest for a few more days?'

Lady Gayle sat on the edge of her bed and tilted her head to one side, regarding Alice with a faint smile. 'I don't think you need to fuss so much, Alice,' she said. 'Dr Sloane simply said I need to convalesce in warmer climes. That's why we're here. I'm just going to take a quick dip and then relax in the sun. I'm sure I'll be fine.'

'Very good, milady,' said Alice. 'One swimming suit, a thick towel, and a flask of hot soup for afterwards. The Dowager Countess would never forgive me if you were to take ill while we are here.'

Lady Gayle guffawed and then coughed. She rose and took two of the painkillers that Dr Sloane had prescribed, washing them down with a glass of warm water that had been on the nightstand. She avoided catching Alice's eye as she knew her maid's expression would be one of rank disapproval. She pulled a shawl around her shoulders and left the bedroom, making her way to the dining room, where she hoped there would be breakfast.

'Ah, there you are, Gigi,' said Charles. 'We were just going to stroll into the square and get breakfast at one of the cafés.'

'Is there nothing here?' said Lady Gayle.

Charles shook his head. 'No, Count Bianchi has left us with the gardener and a housemaid. That's it. If someone comes calling, we have to answer the door ourselves. The same with cooking. We either eat in a café or restaurant, or we have to cook for ourselves.' He shuddered. 'The very idea.'

Dipping her head, Lady Gayle smiled to herself. 'Charles, have you never had to do anything for yourself at any point in your life?'

'Of course, I have,' he said, 'but it's not as if I *like* doing it.'

'Oh Charles, you really are the giddy limit,' said Lady Gayle. 'The next thing you will tell me is that your man puts the paste on your toothbrush for you.'

Charles sniggered. 'No,' he said. 'That really is something I can manage for myself.'

'Good to hear it. Right, lead on. Let's go and find some breakfast.'

Charles held out his arm, and Lady Gayle slipped her hand in the crook of his elbow. Even at this early hour, the sun held real warmth, and Lady Gayle allowed the shawl to slip from her shoulders.

The restaurant where they had dined the night before

was in darkness, but in the opposite corner of the piazza was a tiny establishment with red gingham tablecloths. Charles made a beeline for it and selected one of the tables outside close to the pavement.

'What would you like to eat, Gayle? I'm going to have coffee and croissants,' he said.

'That sounds divine,' said Lady Gayle. 'Make that two.'

'Could you make it three, actually?' Felicity Makepeace flopped into one of the spare chairs at their table.

'Of course,' said Charles. He raised his hand to beckon a waiter and placed the order. He sat back in his chair, retrieved his silver case, and lit a cigarette. He sighed contentedly as he blew thick smoke into the air.

'How are you feeling today, Lady Gayle?' said Felicity Makepeace. 'Did you fancy a swim?'

'I do, if you don't mind me tagging along with you,' said Lady Gayle. 'I've asked my maid to lay out my swimming togs for me, and she's insisting that I take a flask of hot soup too.'

'Golly gosh,' said Felicity. 'How on earth is she going to get that?'

'I have absolutely no idea,' replied Lady Gayle. 'But I have every faith that she will come up with the goods. She's never let me down.'

'She sounds like an absolute treasure. Has she been with you long? Uncle Richard says staff are very difficult to keep these days. Beatrice finds it impossible to make a maid stay.'

'He's quite right,' said Charles. 'I don't seem to be able to keep a valet above a year.'

'But isn't that because you're so dashed fussy, Charles,' laughed Felicity.

'I don't believe I am,' replied Charles with a sniff.

The waiter returned with plates of croissants and coffee. He laid cups and saucers on the table. Charles reached forward and moved the teaspoon to the right-hand side of his coffee cup.

'There,' said Felicity triumphantly. 'That's exactly what I mean. Even the teaspoon wasn't in the right place for you. You're incredibly fussy, Charles. I consider myself to have had a lucky escape.'

Charles flushed but said nothing.

Not knowing quite where to look, Lady Gayle picked up her coffee cup and took a sip. *Where is the woman who was so enamoured of Charles last year?* Still, she thought to herself, it was better than watching Felicity moon over him like a lovelorn calf.

'You don't keep staff yourself, Felicity?' she said.

Felicity shook her head fervently. 'Uncle Richard's allowance doesn't run to that,' she said. 'And I think a lady's maid wouldn't really approve of the racing circuit.'

'No, I suppose not. It must be very exciting though.' Lady Gayle took a bite of the flaky croissant and closed her eyes at the buttery flavour. When she opened her eyes again, she saw that Felicity had chomped through both her croissants and was licking her finger, dabbing up the flaky crumbs from her plate. She reached across the table and took a cigarette from Charles' case.

Lady Gayle expected some minor protest from him at this lack in manners, but he merely passed her his lighter. She looked from one to the other. They are more like brother and sister than ex-lovers, she mused. Where was the furiously jealous young woman that Lady Sylvia had told her about? All this jovial camaraderie was most odd.

'That was absolutely scrummy.' Felicity rose, stubbing out the cigarette and pushing back her chair. She reached into the pocket of her britches and pulled out some crumpled notes, which she dropped on the table. 'Swim time?'

'Indeed,' said Lady Gayle. She stood too, placed a couple of notes on the table and followed Felicity's rapid steps back to the villa.

Conversation was impossible on the journey to the mountain lake. Once there, Lady Gayle's breath was too taken in by the view to want to break the silence. The mountains reached down to the edge of the lake, apart from the small beach where Felicity parked her Bugatti.

After a brief swim in the freezing cold water, they lay on towels, enjoying the sun and the cloudless sky. 'This is absolute bliss,' said Lady Gayle. 'Don't any of the others come up here?'

'No, thank goodness,' drawled Felicity. 'Bea never, ever gets up until after lunch and Uncle Richard is too engrossed in work to want to enjoy the scenery.'

'He seems very young to be your uncle,' remarked Lady Gayle.

'He's not a proper uncle. He's my father's cousin or second cousin. Something like that. At least he let me access some of my money to buy Bugle.' Felicity nodded in the direction of the Bugatti. 'He's got his hand on the purse strings until I'm twenty-five or get married. I don't get the bulk of my fortune until then. Unless he dies, of course. If he dies, then there's no one else to be my guardian, and I get my money then.'

'It seems rather an odd arrangement,' said Lady Gayle. 'Are you not tempted to marry?'

Felicity snorted in a most unladylike manner. 'I am not,' she said. 'Are you?'

'No, but then my financial independence isn't reliant on marriage,' said Lady Gayle.

'True,' replied Felicity, 'but who says marriage will give me financial independence?'

Lady Gayle nodded. The younger woman was right, of course.

CHAPTER SIX

The next couple of days passed in the same fashion—breakfast at the café, a swim and a picnic lunch followed by dinner in the square. Charles began to complain that their days were becoming rather dull. So, it was no surprise that by the time they returned to the villa on the fourth day, he had made plans for the evening's entertainment.

'We are going to have a treasure hunt,' he said, rubbing his hands together. 'After you two departed for your swim, I saw Elizabeth Hansen again. She and that Teddy Devine have sorted out a whole stack of clues. It's going to be tremendous fun. Do say you'll join in?'

'What about cars?' said Felicity. 'Are we going to be one big team, or are we going to split up?'

'Don't worry about that,' said Countess Harding. 'You two can be in one team, and Charles and I will team up. Count Bianchi is going to hunt with Julia Fitzpatrick, but he says Charles can drive one of his spare cars.'

'That's incredibly generous of him,' said Lady Gayle. 'Will Earl Harding not be joining us?'

'Far too much to do,' said Richard Harding as he

accepted a cup of tea and some sandwiches from the housemaid. 'Not all of us live a life of complete leisure, you know.'

Bea Harding flushed, but she seemed to recover quickly before flashing a smile at her husband. 'You work far too hard, my darling,' she gushed. 'Why don't you come and have some fun with the rest of us?'

Richard Harding shook his head and gave his wife a kiss on the cheek before he retired to the room he had taken over as his study.

'Looks as if that means you and I are in one team then, doesn't it?' said Felicity. 'That just leaves the afternoon to fill.'

'How do you fancy trying to fix this fountain?' said Lady Gayle. 'I'm sure it'll be easy enough if we put our heads together.'

'Won't the water get full of green slimy stuff?' asked Charles.

'Oh, ye of little faith, Charles,' said Lady Gayle. 'I was going to ask the gardener if he had something to prevent that. The gardener at Bethencourt Castle puts a copper sulphate solution in the water to stop the build-up of algae. That's the green slimy stuff, Charles.' She gave him a grin.

'There's no need to be quite so smug,' he replied. 'I couldn't quite recall the correct whatchamacallit, the right word.'

'Of course not, Charles,' said Lady Gayle. Turning to Felicity, she said, 'Are you game?'

Felicity nodded enthusiastically, and the two ladies retired to their bedrooms to change into more workmanlike clothing.

Lady Gayle tripped lightly along to her bedroom suite. At the top of the stairs, she hesitated and with a frown, she sniffed the air. Her nose wrinkled at the smell of smoke. It wasn't wood smoke, and in any case, it was far too hot for a fire, but something was being burnt. She shrugged, giving the matter no more consideration, as all her thoughts were focused on the challenge of persuading the old fountain to return to life.

'Turn on the tap please, Giuseppe,' called Lady Gayle. She wiped her hands on a dirty-looking cloth and bit her lip, listening to the gurgling of water undulating through the copper pipes.

Beside her, Felicity tapped her foot on the edge of the stone bowl. The two women reached out and gripped each other's hands as they waited like small children excited for Christmas Day.

The water continued to gurgle, but it was not making an appearance at the head of the fountain.

'Oh, dash it,' said Lady Gayle. 'I thought it was all too easy. Tap off, Giuseppe,' she called.

The gardener nodded from the doorway of a small shed built into the side of the villa's courtyard.

Lady Gayle stood on the stone bowl and reached up to the top of the fountain. She unscrewed a copper spherical object and held it up to her eye. 'Giuseppe, there seems to be a blockage. Have you got something to clear it?'

There was a rummaging sound from the shed, and Giuseppe appeared with something that looked remarkably like a dagger. He passed it, handle forward, to Lady Gayle, and she inserted the tip into the copper ball.

She held the ball to her eye again, then blew through it and inspected it once more before replacing it on top of the fountain. 'Let's give it another go,' she said.

Giuseppe nodded and returned to the shed.

Moments later, Lady Gayle squealed as water gushed from the top of the fountain and tumbled down the tiers into the basin at the bottom. She was soaked, but Felicity grabbed her hands, and together the two women danced around the courtyard.

'Oh, what an absolute whizz you are,' yelled Felicity. She reached her hands forward and rinsed them in the cold water. 'It's going to be lovely to sit out here now.'

Lady Gayle nodded and crossed her arms. She glanced in the direction of the shed and gave Giuseppe a satisfied smile. Nothing made her happier than to resolve a tricky mechanical problem.

Leaving Felicity to delight in the fountain, Lady Gayle went to her bedroom to wash and to change from her damp clothes into something cooler. She was glad she had packed her work britches; even though she'd seen absolutely no reason for bringing them, it was always good to have them close at hand.

Dressed only in her undergarments, she crossed to the window and stared out. Surrounded as it was by the tall cypress trees ubiquitous of Tuscany, she caught glimpses of the village below. Florence, she knew, was in the far distance. Too far away to see any of its stunning architecture. Such a shame, she thought. A breeze caught the light muslin curtain, and Lady Gayle coughed, rubbing her hand against her chest but relieved that the pain was finally subsiding.

'Do you need anything, milady,' said Alice. 'I heard you coughing.'

'I'm fine, thank you, Alice,' said Lady Gayle. 'It was a good idea to come and stay here. I'm feeling much better in the dry weather. I think I will sit by the fountain in the courtyard and perhaps read for a little while.'

'Very good, milady. Will you want a nap before dinner?'

Lady Gayle shook her head. 'No, I feel much, much better,' she said. 'If I'm tired after dinner, then I'm sure they can do the treasure hunt without me.'

Charles brought the first clue, encased in a thick white envelope, to dinner. He placed it in the centre of the table without letting anyone see the contents. All the same, he and Countess Beatrice sat with their heads together, whispering animatedly all throughout the meal.

Finally, when dessert was cleared away, he picked up the envelope and removed the card. He held it up for all to see. The countess took the card from him and ran her eyes over the clue. She frowned, placed it back on the table and leaned back in her chair, lips pursed.

Lady Gayle and Felicity glanced at the clue and then at each other with matching shrugs.

'I have nothing,' said Lady Gayle.

'Me neither,' replied Felicity. 'Perhaps we shouldn't bother?' She held the card over the candle.

'Don't burn it. We can't give up yet; we just need to think for a moment,' said Lady Gayle. 'By the way, did anyone else smell burning earlier on today? I was sure that I could smell someone setting fire to papers.'

Felicity shrugged. 'Not me. Perhaps it was Uncle Richard. He's always very secretive.'

'Nonsense, he's simply careful,' replied Bea Harding, taking the card from Felicity. She peered at the words. 'Now, don't tell me you're stumped by the very first clue, girls? That's not going to be much fun at all.'

Felicity narrowed her eyes and glared at the countess.

Lady Gayle nudged her, 'Come on, we repaired the

fountain. I'm sure we can sort this out easily.' All the same, she ran her eyes over the words handwritten on the card in clear capital letters. Despite her outward confidence, she was wracking her brains.

"Start where the sun sets and head east.
Look for a spot where nature meets the town wall,
That's where you'll find your next clue."

What on earth can that mean, she wondered. 'Head east is easy, but where does the sun set?'

'The sun sets in the west,' muttered Felicity so softly that Lady Gayle struggled to hear her. 'But it's not in one place, is it?'

'No.' Lady Gayle took the card and read the words again and again. 'I've had an idea, but I'll tell you when we're on our own.'

Felicity giggled, holding her forefinger over her lips. 'Mum's the word.'

CHAPTER SEVEN

After dinner, Lady Gayle and Felicity wrapped up in warm coats and ran outside to the Bugatti.

'What did you work out?' said Felicity.

'Remember when we went out to eat the other night?'

Felicity nodded.

'Well, I noticed that the spire on top of the church hits the town wall when the sun sets behind it—'

'—and you think?'

'I do,' replied Lady Gayle. 'Shall we?'

They jumped into the car, and Felicity powered up the engine. The two ladies raced away from the villa in wreaths of laughter.

Lady Gayle had been right. As soon as the sun tumbled from the sky, the shadow of the spire hit the town wall. Felicity scrabbled around the base of the wall but found nothing.

'Blast,' she said. 'We can't be right. Read it again.'

Lady Gayle looked down at the slip of paper that she'd

copied the clue onto. 'What about on the other side of the wall? Does nature meet the wall on the other side?'

Felicity stared open-mouthed for a moment. 'Of course.' She dashed through the gap where the remnants of an ancient door hung from one hinge. Lady Gayle followed, and as they rounded the corner, they saw Lady Hansen and Teddy Devine rushing away in the opposite direction.

Felicity pounced on the card they had left behind. It was the next clue.

"In the park, where people relax and play.
In David's hand,
the next clue is hidden away."

'David's hand?' muttered Felicity. 'David who? Is he always in the park? Doesn't he have a home to go to?'

Lady Gayle closed her eyes, recalling the travel guide she'd glanced at on the train. 'Michelangelo's David,' she said. 'The real one is in Florence in the Academia Gallery, but I think there are copies in various towns in the region.'

'But isn't he supposed to be seventeen feet tall. How are we going to reach his hands?'

Lady Gayle laughed, 'I have no idea. Let's just hope this one is a little shorter. Come on.'

Felicity flashed her a glance with pursed lips, but all the same, she drove to the park by the river, which flowed from the mountain lake where they had swum only that morning. As they jumped out the car and approached the bronzed copy of the David, Teddy Devine waved the card on which was written the next clue at them.

To their shock and chagrin, he tore the card into small pieces and tossed those in the air to be captured by the breeze.

'What a ghastly cheat,' said Felicity.

'What's happened?' Charles Vickery and Bea Harding joined them, and together the four hunters gathered up the remains of the card.

The countess pieced the remnants together on the statue's base. Her face had taken on a grey pallor, and she was breathing heavily; she looked absolutely furious.

'Dashed childish to rip it up like that,' said Charles. 'It's hard enough without making it a jigsaw puzzle too.'

'It certainly is,' said Lady Gayle. She glanced at Bea Harding with concern but was relieved to see that the countess had recovered her temper. 'I can't make head nor tail of this last clue, can you, Felicity?'

Felicity looked at the words and shrugged. 'This funny spiky handwriting makes it quite hard to read,' she said. 'The library? What does that mean? There isn't a public library here, is there?'

Lady Gayle perused the card and looked at the other team. 'I think I give up. I'm getting a bit cold.'

'We'll carry on, won't we, Charles?' Bea was staring up at Charles as if daring him to disagree. She pulled at his arm, bringing his head down towards hers, and she whispered in his ear.

Charles nodded, 'We'll be off,' he said, holding out his arm to Bea.

She slipped her hand into the crook of his elbow, and they sauntered away.

'Are we going back to the villa?' said Felicity.

'Can we find some cosy little bar? I'm not ready to go back, but I am fed up with chasing around.'

'I know just the place. Come along.' Felicity held her elbow out in a parody of Charles' gesture, and together they strolled back to the Bugatti.

Although Felicity left her car in the main piazza, she crossed the square and slipped down a small road which was scarcely wider than a passageway. It was certainly too narrow for a car. The entire street was in darkness, then was suddenly flooded with light as a pair of doors opened onto the street. Two unsteady patrons were disgorged, the doors closed, and the street became dark once more. Felicity marched up to the double doors and rapped what could only be a signal.

A panel in the door shot back, was slid into place and the doors opened again. Taking a moment to become used to the bright lights, Lady Gayle blinked before taking a look around. On a raised stage, a ragtime band was playing. A slender, dark-skinned woman swayed in time to the music as she clung to a microphone stand. Her eyes were on the band leader, not her audience. He lowered his trombone, and she began to croon a popular melody. Making her way across the crowded floor to a spare table, Lady Gayle felt the music creep into her soul. The woman's voice was magical. The music faded for a moment and began again as the singer started a new song. Her words were powerful and redolent with meaning.

'I've not heard this song before.' Lady Gayle leaned across the table to whisper to Felicity.

You wouldn't have,' replied Felicity. 'Lots of the songs she sings, she writes herself.' With closed eyes, Felicity swayed in time with the singer, until a man came over and asked her to dance. Irritated, Felicity waved him away. 'I want to listen,' was all she said.

A waiter brought over cocktails that they had not

ordered. Lady Gayle searched the room for someone waiting for thanks and acknowledgement, but the waiter leaned down. 'These are Miss Makepeace's own concoction. I took the liberty of bringing you the same, but I can bring you something else if you prefer.'

Lady Gayle picked up the glass and took a sip. 'Oh no, this is absolutely divine. I'll stick with this, thank you.'

The waiter nodded and withdrew. When the singer finished her song, Felicity opened her eyes, downed the drink, and waved at the waiter. The singer slid into a chair at their table.

'Janie, this is Lady Gayle Summer. Gayle, this is Miss Jane Blues. Songstress extraordinaire.'

Jane tittered, holding her hand over her mouth. 'I just sing with the voice God gave me.'

'You were amazing,' said Lady Gayle. 'I've never heard anything like it. It's as if you saw into my heart and sang what you found there.' Lady Gayle's hands flew to her cheeks. It must be the cocktail, she thought. She had never ever been so frank about what she was thinking.

'It's a universal story of any woman who's ever been in love,' replied Janie. 'Loving them and losing them. That's all I sing about.' She fell silent but gave Felicity a meaningful glance.

'Janie has a problem,' said Felicity. 'That's why I wanted her to meet you. I told her you could help.'

Lady Gayle regarded Felicity through narrowed slits. 'You did? How did you think I might help?'

'Janie's been swindled. I said we'd get her money back for her.'

'It's not me who was swindled, but a friend of mine. I told Felicity not to bother you...'

Lady Gayle gulped. She turned to the singer. 'I am so

sorry, Miss Blues. Felicity has given you the wrong idea. I'm not a private detective. I've simply been lucky a couple of times solving puzzles. I'm strictly an amateur.'

'It's no matter.' Jane Blues rose. 'Thank you for your time. I'm glad you liked my song.' The singer strode away, and Lady Gayle watched her leave. As Jane Blues pushed the curtain aside to go backstage, a man grabbed her wrist. Jane pulled away, but he maintained his grip on her. Lady Gayle saw them exchange furious words before Jane was able to extricate herself from his grasp.

The man turned and glanced around at the patrons as if he were wondering if anyone had seen his behaviour. *Perhaps he sensed I was watching?* He tipped his hat to Lady Gayle and dropped the curtain, preventing her from seeing anything else.

CHAPTER EIGHT

Miss Blues returned to the stage and sang a few more of her atmospheric songs. When she left the stage for a break, she did not return to speak to Felicity and Lady Gayle noticed the moue of disappointment on her new friend's face.

Lady Gayle gazed around the club. It was hard to make out the other patrons with the smoky haze which hung over the individual tables. It was similar to some of the jazz clubs in London she'd visited during and after the war. Without the immense dance floor of the Cosmopolitan Club, this bar had a more intimate atmosphere. She wondered how much it was like the speakeasies she'd imagined Charles running in Atlantic City.

She glanced at Felicity, who was staring forlornly at her drink. 'Do you want to leave?'

'No, I want another drink.' Felicity twisted in her seat and signalled the waiter. She ordered them more cocktails, but Lady Gayle declined, deciding that water might be a better bet.

'Where did you meet Jane?'

'Monte,' replied Felicity. 'I was there during the winter, training for the rally, and she was dating one of the other drivers. We found we had a lot in common.'

Monte Carlo thought Lady Gayle with a sigh. Somewhere she still wanted to visit. 'You both lead very exciting lives. I can't imagine what's more fun: being a racing driver or a nightclub singer.'

Felicity shrugged. She stared at the curtain which covered the entrance to the backstage area. After a few moments of hopeless gazing, she drank her cocktail in two gulps and ordered another.

'Shouldn't we go back to the villa?' said Lady Gayle.

Felicity nodded. 'Very well.' She pushed herself away from the table and rose unsteadily, peering around and blinking.

Oh, good grief, she's far too drunk to drive. Lady Gayle closed the gap to Felicity's side rapidly before Felicity slid to the floor. She pushed her way under Felicity's arm and made the younger woman use her as support. Together, they staggered from the club into the darkened street. Using the wall for her own support, Lady Gayle manoeuvred the very drunk driver back towards the car. She opened the passenger door and pushed Felicity inside the vehicle. She went around to the driver's side and pushed the starter button. Nothing happened.

'Now, how on earth do I start this thing?' Lady Gayle glanced at the now snoring Felicity. Even if she could wake her companion, she wasn't likely to be much use. Crankshaft it is then, thought Lady Gayle. She reached around on the back seat, found the crank shaft, and alighted to put it in place. It took a couple of turns, but she soon had the engine rumbling contentedly. She rose and placed the crankshaft in the boot. As she dropped the lid, she saw Jane

Blues dashing across the street. Lady Gayle raised her hand to wave but quickly dropped it. There was something about the way Miss Blues' head was darting around; it gave the impression she didn't want to be seen. *What is she up to?*

Lady Gayle turned her attention to Felicity while allowing the engine to warm. She made sure the younger woman wasn't going to be ill; then she drove them back to the villa.

As she eased the powerful car into the courtyard, Felicity woke and looked around in surprise. 'We're back,' she said.

'Well spotted,' murmured Lady Gayle. 'Do you need me to get you to your bed, or can you manage?'

'Bed? It's not time for bed, is it? I want another drink.' She staggered out of the car straight into Charles' arms.

He raised his eyebrows at Lady Gayle. 'You look like you two have had fun, Gigi.'

'She got a bit upset about something. Nothing serious. She'll be fine after a good night's sleep. Perhaps you could give me a hand getting her to her room.'

'Of course,' said Charles.

'Where's Bea?'

'I'm here. What happened to you two?'

Lady Gayle noticed that Countess Beatrice had changed her frock. She dipped her head and quickly looked away. It was none of her business what her fellow guests got up to in private.

'Charles spilt champagne all over me,' drawled Bea as if in reply to her glance. 'I had to change.'

'Champagne,' murmured Felicity. 'I'd like some champagne.'

'I think you've had enough,' said Lady Gayle.

'Spoilsport.' Felicity hiccoughed and slid through Charles' arms.

'Let me carry her through to the courtyard chairs, and I'll get another bottle,' said Charles. 'I'll pour her a drop, otherwise she'll only kick up a fuss.'

'Very well,' replied Lady Gayle. She moved towards the courtyard and the fountain. Then she halted, having almost collided with Bea, who had frozen in place. As she glanced at Bea, the countess screeched in shock.

Lying head down in the stone basin at the foot of the fountain was a man. Charles placed Felicity on the ground and ran over to the man, removed his head from the water and rolled him over onto his back.

It was Earl Richard Harding, and he wasn't moving. Countess Bea sucked in a lungful of air, and the night was rent with her screams.

Charles rose, leaving Richard where he lay and dashed to her side. 'Bea, calm down,' he said.

Lady Gayle sighed. She always found it so frustrating when people told others to calm down. It never had the desired impact in her experience, and today was no exception.

Countess Bea continued screaming whilst Charles clutched her shoulders. His expression was one of complete bewilderment. Yet the woman had just found her husband dead, Lady Gayle's heart squeezed in sympathy for her angst.

Felicity, still unable to stand, started to crawl towards the fountain. 'Uncle Richard,' she said. 'Wake up, Uncle Richard.'

Lady Gayle crouched beside her, 'He's not going to wake up, Felicity. I'm sorry, but he's dead.'

'Are you sure?'

'I think so,' replied Lady Gayle. 'Let me check.' She rose and closed the few steps between her and the dead man in seconds. She bent down and pressed her fingers against the inside of his wrist. Feeling nothing, she bit her lip and pressed her fingers beside the bulge of his Adam's apple. Still nothing. She glanced at Charles and shook her head.

Charles continued comforting Bea, his hand on the back of her head, holding her closely. Her screams had subsided into defiant sobs, and he continued to whisper words of comfort to her.

'We need to call the police,' Lady Gayle said.

'Are you sure it wasn't an accident?' hissed Charles.

Lady Gayle put her hands on her hips and stared at him. 'We need to call the police and let Count Bianchi know.'

'Let Count Bianchi know what?'

Lady Gayle whirled around. Count Bianchi strolled into the courtyard with the blonde woman from the night before on his arm. The newcomers took in the scene without comment.

Their cold demeanour was chilling. *Don't they care? Or isn't it a surprise?* Lady Gayle glowered at them; her mind was buzzing with questions.

'I think we might all need a drink,' said Julia Fitzpatrick. Without asking for directions, she headed into the villa, returning promptly with a bottle of cognac and several glasses.

While Julia poured and offered brandy to everyone, Count Bianchi woke the gardener and sent him for the local constable.

Lady Gayle sipped the warming liquid while they stood

around, looking helplessly at Earl Harding's body. Charles had taken Countess Beatrice into the sitting room to keep her warm after the shock of finding her husband's body. Felicity had been put to bed by Julia, who seemed to know her way around the villa extremely well.

'I've left a large glass of water by her bed and a bowl on the floor,' she said as she rejoined the group.

'Thank you,' murmured Lady Gayle. 'You didn't have to do that.'

Julia shrugged but didn't reply.

All heads turned at the sound of a car racing towards the villa. Expecting the police to turn up, they were all rather surprised to see Teddy Devine and Lady Hansen skid to a halt in a smart two-seater. Elizabeth Hansen cuddled a jeroboam of champagne in her arms like a baby. 'I rather think we won,' she announced.

CHAPTER NINE

No one spoke immediately. Lady Hansen lowered the oversized champagne bottle onto her seat and pulled at the door handle. Teddy Devine leapt out the driver's seat and was swiftly at her side opening the car door for her.

'What's happened?' he drawled, chewing on a large cigar.

Lady Hansen wobbled around the end of the car and took in the scene.

Oh, goodness, she's going to scream too, thought Lady Gayle. Her ears hadn't quite recovered from the noise of Countess Beatrice's screams. She stiffened in preparation, but no sound came.

Lady Hansen edged closer; her eyes rounded, but apart from a sharp intake of breath, she seemed perfectly calm. 'He's dead, I take it?'

Lady Gayle nodded, 'Yes, I've checked. He's quite dead. Count Bianchi has sent the gardener to fetch the police.'

Lady Hansen dipped her head but still accepted a glass of cognac from Julia Fitzpatrick. Julia glanced at Teddy Devine and shrugged.

The gestures did not go unnoticed by Lady Gayle. Whatever it meant, they seemed mildly irritated by Earl Harding's death rather than shocked or saddened. She gazed around at the group, taking in the expressions on everyone's faces. While she was making a mental note of everything she could see, she shivered. A shawl was slipped around her shoulders, and her notebook and pencil were thrust into her hands.

Lady Gayle smiled at Alice, who had silently appeared by her side. 'Thank you,' she whispered. 'How did you know?'

'I heard the commotion, but Lord Charles came to ask me to take care of the countess,' murmured Alice. 'I just came out to see what was going on.'

'I think Earl Harding has been murdered.' Lady Gayle edged away from the group, and Alice followed. It would not do to voice her opinions within earshot of the others. However, before she could say anything more, there was a jangle of a bell, and a small black car hurtled through the gates.

Giuseppe, the gardener, alighted from the rear of the vehicle. A short, plump man struggled to remove himself from the passenger seat. He straightened his uniform and reached inside the car for his cap. He ran his gaze over the assembled group and sauntered towards them.

A second police officer clambered from the driver's seat; he too, straightened his uniform but stayed next to the car.

'I am Constable Matteo Ferri,' said the first policeman, tugging his jacket down over a paunch. His large stomach put his polished brass buttons under a tremendous strain. He glanced in the direction of Count Bianchi and gave a small bow. 'What has happened here?'

Lady Gayle noticed that he directed his question only to Count Bianchi, ignoring the other people gathered.

'I was not here,' the count replied. 'There are other, better witnesses present, however.' He waved his hand to include everyone gathered around.

Constable Ferri glanced about at the assembled group. 'You,' he said to Lord Charles, 'what can you tell me?'

'Not very much, I'm afraid.' Charles stepped closer to the squat police officer. 'We came back after our treasure hunt and found his Grace in the fountain, dead as a doornail.'

Constable Ferri looked up at Charles and then took a step back. 'What about you?' he said to Teddy Devine.

Teddy shrugged and chewed on his cigar. 'I just arrived. I don't know any more than you do.'

'Surely someone must know something,' Constable Ferri growled. 'Someone must have seen something. Who are the witnesses?'

Lady Gayle coughed, and the constable turned his head towards her.

'Yes, you may go, signorina,' he said. 'All the ladies may go. I might have questions later, but in the meantime, I must find out what happened here.'

Count Bianchi snorted with laughter. 'You are surrounded by witnesses, Constable,' he said. 'If you could but see it. Lady Gayle was the first back after the treasure hunt with Countess Harding. They found the body.'

Constable Ferri flushed and glowered at the count. 'I think we should go indoors.' He turned to Giuseppe and told him to stay with the Earl's body. 'Touch nothing,' he warned. Then, with a bow to the ladies, he indicated that they should return to the villa.

Lady Gayle and Alice were at the back of the group. 'I

see we have our work cut out here, milady,' murmured Alice.

'Oh Alice, I quite agree. Never did you speak a truer word.'

When they were gathered in the drawing room, everyone began to speak at once. Count Bianchi called for calm but was ignored. It wasn't until Constable Ferri blew his whistle that a shocked silence fell.

'Order,' he shouted. 'I must have order. I will speak to you all one at a time in a separate area. Who found the body?'

Lady Gayle raised her hand. She felt as if she was back at school. 'I was with Countess Harding when we came across her husband's body. She is still rather shocked, I'm afraid. She is lying down in her room.'

'Then I will speak to you first,' he said. 'We need to find another place to speak privately.' He opened the drawing room door, and Lady Gayle strolled through it. The kitchen was probably the best place to talk she thought, and she led the way there.

In the kitchen, she sat at the scrubbed table, and the constable took a seat opposite. She answered all the standard questions about what she had seen and heard. She was surprised that he didn't ask about her suspicions, but she had to remind herself he wasn't Detective Inspector Coward. In fact, as far as she could tell, he wasn't a detective at all. *Perhaps that's why he's not asking the right questions.* When she was dismissed—that was the only word she could think of to describe it—she returned to the drawing room.

Alice was no longer in attendance, and Lady Gayle

thought perhaps that her maid had returned upstairs. She sat sipping cognac and half-listening to the conversation around her. She was on the point of asking Charles how Countess Harding was when the lady returned to the room. She was pale-faced after her questioning, and Alice slipped, unnoticed by everyone else, into the room.

Lady Gayle glanced at her maid, who was nodding urgently in the direction of their quarters upstairs.

'I say, Gigi, old thing,' drawled Charles. 'I think you should go with your maid before her head falls off.'

Giving him a quick glower, Lady Gayle took his advice and followed Alice.

'What's so urgent,' she hissed at Alice once they were alone, 'and where did you get to?'

'I was in the kitchen,' replied Alice.

Lady Gayle frowned. 'How did you get away with that? Didn't the constable ask you to leave?'

Alice grinned and shook her head. 'I thought he might tell me to go, but when I saw how he treated you ladies, I did wonder if he'd be as dismissive of servants too. It turns out I was right.'

'Did you hide?'

'Oh no, milady,' said Alice. 'I simply hovered at the sink and washed a few glasses. I don't think he knew I was there. But I heard everything.'

Lady Gayle inhaled sharply and then biting back a paroxysm of coughing, wished she hadn't. 'Tell me?'

'Countess Harding just lied to that policeman,' said Alice. 'She said to us that she and Lord Charles were back first, and she had gone up to her room to change her dress, didn't she?'

Lady Gayle nodded. 'Charles spilt champagne on her dress, so she had to change.'

'Well, she's just told the constable that she returned with Lord Charles and was with him right up until the body was found. And what's more, he believed her.'

CHAPTER TEN

'Oh dear, lying to the police is never a good idea,' said Lady Gayle. 'But she does have an alibi since she was with Lord Charles when the Earl was murdered.'

'Was she, milady? Are you quite sure?'

Lady Gayle shook her head. 'No, I'm not completely positive, but I saw how taken aback she was when she found Earl Harding's body.' She closed her eyes for a moment, trying to fathom what she was forgetting. *Of course,* she snapped her eyes open and stared at her maid. 'I smelt paper burning when I came back from my swim earlier today. I didn't think anything of it at the time, and when I mentioned it to the others, no one knew what I was talking about. Yet someone must have been trying to hide something.'

'Which room was the smell coming from, milady?'

'I'm not sure. I can't quite remember. I was standing at the top of the stairs; it could have been any of the rooms on that corridor.'

'Think hard, milady,' said Alice. 'We can always go and stand in the corridor so you can retrace your steps.'

Lady Gayle nodded. 'That's a very good idea, Alice.' She rose and opened her bedroom door, sneaking a peek up and down the corridor to make sure they were alone. She slipped out of the bedroom and strolled to the top of the stairs. Placing her hand on the bannister, Lady Gayle closed her eyes and thought back to the time just a few hours before.

Earl and Countess Harding had their adjoining bedrooms just to the left of the stairway. To the right were the rooms where Lady Gayle and Alice slept. Immediately opposite their suite were Felicity's rooms. Lord Charles had been placed in a room on the floor above.

Unsure of which way to go, Lady Gayle nibbled her lip for a moment. The smell had been stronger at the top of the stairs, and it had dissipated by the time she reached her own room. She glanced at Felicity's bedroom door but shook her head.

'This way,' she said, beckoning to Alice. 'We'll go this way.'

She crept along the corridor and listened for a moment at Countess Harding's door. Satisfied that there was no one within, she pushed down the iron door handle and eased the door open. She peeked into the room and, finding it empty, she stepped over the threshold, beckoning Alice to follow.

'I don't like this, milady,' Alice said, easing the bedroom door closed. She stayed beside the door, darting glances around the room as if she expected someone to leap from the wardrobe at any moment.

'I know. I understand, but I need you to listen out to see if anyone is coming.' Lady Gayle moved softly around the room. She hesitated by the window where Bea Harding's dress was hanging. Drops of moisture were dripping from the dress. She leaned towards it and gave it a sniff. 'That doesn't smell like champagne,' she said.

'Perhaps she rinsed it out, milady. Otherwise, the dress could have been left with a nasty stain.'

'Yes, you're right, of course.' Lady Gayle edged towards the fireplace and picked up the poker. With the tip of the poker, she moved around burnt pieces of paper in the grate. 'Everything is burnt to a crisp. That's a nuisance.' She dropped to her knees and peered into the fireplace. With one hand on the hearth, she pulled out the fire front and, with the fire tongs, she retrieved a small, unburnt slip of paper. Turning it over in her hand, she spotted the end of one word and the start of another scrawled in spidery writing.

'I've seen this writing somewhere before,' she said to Alice.

'Is it Lord Charles' handwriting?' said Alice.

Lady Gayle shook her head, 'No, it looks like a woman's writing. And I've seen it quite recently.'

'I think someone is coming,' hissed Alice. 'It's time for us to leave.'

Lady Gayle rose and carefully folded the small piece of paper in her handkerchief. She was only just in time, as the door was thrust open, and Bea Harding stood on the threshold.

'What on earth are you two doing in here?' she demanded. 'How dare you invade my privacy like this. What do you think you're up to?'

'I thought I heard a noise,' said Lady Gayle. 'Something in the chimney. So, I called my maid to help.'

'A likely story,' hissed the Countess. She crossed the room quickly and, pushing Lady Gayle aside, she squinted up the chimney. 'If there was anything, there's nothing there now. I'd like you to leave.'

'Yes, of course,' said Lady Gayle. 'We'll leave you in peace unless you want to talk or have someone sit with you. Especially after your terrible shock?'

'I'd like to be left alone, thank you. Please close the door behind you.'

Lady and maid exchanged glances and left. On the point of returning to their own suite, they hesitated. Constable Ferri swaggered up the stairs. He was followed by the second constable, who was pulling handcuffs from his belt. Ferri waved a half-burnt letter in his left hand. He marched to Countess Harding's door and hammered on it until it creaked open.

'Explain to me this, Countess Harding,' shouted Ferri through the crack. 'What do you know about this letter we found in your husband's jacket?'

Lady Gayle was on the point of stepping forward to protest when she felt Alice's hand on her forearm.

'There's nothing we can do just now, milady,' she whispered. 'Perhaps we can organise a solicitor for her?'

'Good idea,' replied Lady Gayle in a low voice. 'I'm sure that's something Charles can arrange, or perhaps the name of their local man is in amongst Earl Harding's papers.'

Just at that moment, the door opened, and Countess Harding, her wrists bound behind her in the manacles, was led from her room and down the stairs.

'I'm innocent, Lady Gayle,' she called. 'You must believe me. Can you telegram our solicitor? Mr Buckingham in Greys Inn.'

'You can rely on me, Bea,' Lady Gayle called down the stairs. 'I won't let you down.' She stared as Bea Harding was led away. When she reached the foot of the stairs, the other guests were all milling around open-mouthed as the Countess was placed in the rear of the small black car.

The bell jangled once more as the police officers and the reluctant countess raced away into the night.

As the sound of the bell faded into the distance, everyone returned to the villa's drawing room. Even Felicity had arisen and was listening to a resume of recent events from Charles. She still looked the worse for wear, but the shock had sobered her up considerably.

'I'll dig out Mr Buckingham's details,' she offered. 'They'll be in Uncle Richard's papers. I know where he keeps most things.' She turned towards the room Earl Harding had been using for his study and halted. 'Kept,' was all she said. Charles followed her.

In the silence that followed, Lady Gayle poured herself a half glass of champagne and strolled out into the courtyard. Count Bianchi stood by the fountain, chatting with his gardener. Earl Harding's body remained in situ. The count blew thick white smoke from his cigar into the still night. He turned when Giuseppe indicated her presence.

'Ah, Lady Gayle, please allow me to offer my most abject apologies. This must have been quite a shock for you.'

'Less than you might imagine, Count Bianchi,' she murmured. She decided against giving him any further details. There was every chance he'd find out in due course. 'The police found something in Earl Harding's pockets, I take it?'

The count nodded and puffed another cloud of smoke into the atmosphere. 'A letter. From a lady,' he said. 'A lady who was not his wife.'

'I see. Do you know which lady?'

The count nodded, but he didn't offer up a name. 'I wait now for the good *dottore* to arrive and take my dear friend Earl Harding away, and then I shall go for my bed.'

The correction was on the tip of her tongue, but it seemed neither the time nor the place to offer English lessons. 'I didn't realise you were so close to the Earl. I am sorry for your loss.'

The count bowed briefly but said nothing.

Lady Gayle kept her face impassive as she thought back to the count's cold demeanour when they'd found Earl Harding's body. She shivered. 'I think I'll go to bed too. Good night, Count Bianchi. Good night, Giuseppe.'

Both men nodded. As she walked away, Lady Gayle was surprised to hear them conversing in rapid-fire Italian. It sounded urgent and not at all like Giuseppe was expressing his condolences to his employer.

What on earth was that all about, she wondered.

CHAPTER ELEVEN

BREAKFAST THE FOLLOWING MORNING WAS A SUBDUED AFFAIR. Charles had visited the café and ordered coffee and croissants to be delivered. They were every bit as delicious as the day before but were not eaten with the same enthusiasm as on previous days.

Count Bianchi arrived in the middle of the morning. He did not bring good news.

'La contessa remains with the police,' he began.

'How long can they keep her under arrest,' demanded Felicity. 'She's innocent. She would never kill Uncle Richard. They adored each other. They must have other suspects.'

The count nodded. 'A militia commander will be here later today. He will take charge of the investigation.'

'A militia commander?' said Charles, drawing his brows together. 'Doesn't that make him a Blackshirt? What jurisdiction does he have over a civil case amongst foreigners?'

The count raised his hands, palms uppermost to mid-chest, then lowered them slowly. 'My dear Lord Charles, there has been a murder, which is a criminal case, not civil, and we do not let murderers walk free just because they are visitors in my country.

'I agree that a member of the militia taking over the case is unusual, but he was a detective before the war, and I am told he is a very experienced investigator. I can assure you he is the best man for the job. I urge you all to give him your utmost help and cooperation.'

'You can count on us, Count,' said Charles, grinning at his own pun.

Count Bianchi looked to the heavens. Presumably for guidance or perhaps patience. 'I am very grateful, Lord Charles,' he said. 'I am sure that Commander Ricciardi will be too. Now, I must leave you all. I have my house guests at my other villa to whom I must attend. *Ciao*.' He rose and gave the ladies a small bow, shook hands with Charles, and with a smoothing of his grey moustache, he left.

'Where did Julia Fitzpatrick go last night?' Felicity began. 'One minute she was there putting me to bed, and the next she was gone.'

'You remember that, do you?' said Charles. 'She retired after she was questioned. She walked back to Villa de Colli with Lizzie and Teddy. They hadn't seen anything, so the constable didn't have questions for them.'

'He nearly didn't have questions for people who *had* seen things,' retorted Lady Gayle. 'I'm glad he won't be investigating the case.'

'He was the one who found the letter in Richard's jacket pocket,' said Charles mildly. 'That's why Bea was taken to the police station.'

'Do you know who the letters were from? Or what they said. The count was very discreet last night, which is always irritating in an investigation.'

'Why can't you leave well alone, Gigi? You can't investigate this as one of your cases.'

'I can and I will. Mostly because Bea begged me to help her last night. I wasn't very keen on the way she spoke to me when I arrived, but she was desperate last night, and I made her a promise. So come on, Charles. What was in the letters?'

'They were letters from a lady to her lover.'

'The lover being Earl Harding?'

Charles nodded.

'And the lady?'

Felicity snorted. 'This is all stuff and nonsense,' she said. 'Utter tommyrot.'

Lady Gayle glanced at her. 'You sound very sure.'

'Look, I spent a lot of time with them both. They were devoted to each other. If they weren't, then I would have spotted it. Stands to reason.'

Lady Gayle nodded. Since Felicity was Richard Harding's niece of sorts, she frequently stayed with the couple. She saw them as few others did. However, no one really knew what went on between husband and wife behind closed doors. Would Felicity have known the truth or not?

'Countess Harding told me the same yesterday,' said Lady Gayle, watching Felicity's face carefully. 'I don't think I'll believe in the existence of a lover until I see some hard evidence. Who else had Earl Harding upset? What about his businesses? Was everything on the up and up?'

Charles coughed, and Felicity patted him on the back. 'Steady on there, old chap,' she said. 'Can't have you dropping off your perch too.'

Charles looked affronted at the thought. 'I am perfectly well,' he said. 'How much business news do you follow?'

Lady Gayle and Felicity exchanged glances. 'None,' they said in unison.

'Best you both pin back your ears, then,' said Charles. 'I have a story to tell, but I suggest I don't tell it here. Let's go to the café after all.'

'Have either of you heard of the Imperial Ventures Group?' Charles said when they were all settled.

Both shook their heads.

'Very well, it was a company set up in America, just after the war, for people to invest capital into a number of different companies. The idea was to give the companies a boost after the war and give them access to capital that they would otherwise struggle to raise themselves.'

'What kind of people had money to invest after the war?' said Lady Gayle.

Charles cocked his head to one side and raised an eyebrow.

'Very well, and how did Imperial Ventures Group perform for these war profiteers? Was it successful?' asked Lady Gayle.

Charles shook his head. 'It was not a success,' he said. 'Very far from it, sadly. It worked well at first, but after a while, there were very few returns on profit. That's when they began looking for alternative investors and looked to English businessmen.'

'Did your Mr Bishop get involved?' asked Lady Gayle referring to Charles' late business partner and benefactor.

'John was approached, but after some consideration of their offer, he declined. Earl Harding did not decline, however, but I suspect he wished later that he had. He got in deep, and there was no way out for him. In fact, there was so very little profit that eventually Richard was paying dividends to shareholders out of the money he received from new investors.'

'Isn't that rather risky?' said Felicity.

'Risky and stupid,' said Charles. 'In the end, you're simply robbing Peter to pay Paul all the time. Eventually, the bubble bursts.'

'Is it legal?' asked Lady Gayle

'Not exactly legal and not illegal as such, although questions have been asked about it in the Houses of Parliament. There are those who would like to see it made illegal as it's gambling with people's money when the investors think they are placing their money in something solid.'

'So, it *is* fraudulent?'

'It is,' said Charles, nodding and blowing out the last of the smoke from his cigarette.

'And how do you know so much about it,' asked Lady Gayle.

Charles smashed the cigarette stub into the bottom of the ashtray. He ground it to a fine powder before answering. 'I was involved at one point but decided to put my money to work elsewhere.'

'How did Earl Harding feel about that?'

Charles stared at Lady Gayle before answering. 'I don't think he was in so deep when I walked away. That may have changed.'

'He's been worried about money and business ever since we arrived,' said Felicity. 'I think he was trying to persuade Count Bianchi to invest.'

Charles laughed. 'Bianchi is far too wily an old bird to invest with Harding.'

'He won't have lost money then,' said Lady Gayle. 'That's good news. We can take him off the list. I thought people who'd lost money might feel they had a justifiable reason to murder Earl Harding.'

Charles groaned. 'Honestly, Gigi, you have to listen to me,' he said. 'You really must leave it to the police this time.'

'Impossible,' she replied with a shake of her head. 'They think Bea is guilty. They won't look for anyone else. We will at least consider all the other options. You know me, I see a thread, and I have to pull at it until I see the whole truth. Can you think of anyone else who lost money with this company of Earl Harding's?'

'I can't,' Charles said, reclining in his chair. 'However, I do not believe that it was Earl Harding's company. He came on board around the time I left. That's why there were no hard feelings between us. I do, however, feel that he was invited to become a director to lend an air of respectability to the company.'

'Were you not respectable enough, Charles?' asked Felicity with a grin.

'Probably not. I'm a mere viscount. That's nothing compared to an Earl. I don't sit in the House of Lords, for example. I leave all that to Pater.'

'How is your father?' said Lady Gayle. It was rare for Charles to mention the lovely old man who was his father.

'Oh, he trundles along. The House, his club and back home to Gloucestershire every so often. He'll outlive us all. You see if he doesn't.'

Lady Gayle gave a faint smile. She caught the eye of the waiter and ordered more coffee. When it arrived, the waiter poured refills for everyone and returned to his post in the shade of an awning. Lady Gayle thought back to Alice's comment the previous night about staff being invisible. 'There has to be someone,' she said. 'Someone we've ignored or not considered. We were all out on the treasure hunt. Perhaps someone came to the villa to see Lord Harding. Do we know?'

'The only person who would know is dead,' remarked Charles. 'The housemaid doesn't stay after seven in the evening. If anyone called after she left, then Richard would have had to let them in himself.'

'What about the gardener?' said Lady Gayle. 'Where does he sleep? Or Earl Harding's valet? Wouldn't he let a caller in?'

'You're asking the wrong person, Gigi,' said Charles. 'I really don't know much about the private lives of below stairs.'

'Charles, you're an incorrigible snob. It's about time you did learn.'

Charles, however, was not listening. His attention was drawn to a tall, dark-haired man striding towards their table.

CHAPTER TWELVE

Lady Gayle followed his gaze. The man marching towards them was dressed entirely in black, from the fez-style hat down to his long black boots. The fascist emblem adorned his black shirt. When he reached them, he stopped and gave a curt bow. 'I am Commander Alessandro Ricciardi. I must ask you some questions.'

'Won't you take a seat, Commander,' Charles drawled, waving his hand towards the spare chair at their table.

'I thank you, but no. Lady Gayle Summer, I presume?' The commander gave another brief bow, snapping the heels of his long boots together. 'Will you accompany me to the police station?'

Lady Gayle was on the point of rising, but Charles held out his hand. 'Don't, Gigi,' he said. To the commander, he said. 'Her ladyship will be going nowhere alone with you. She will need her maid at the very least.'

'Charles, no. Don't be silly, I'll be perfectly safe with the commander,' she said. When she looked into Commander Ricciardi's jet-black eyes, she bit back a breath. His eyes were as bottomless and cold as the well which fed water to Bethencourt Castle. She shuddered. 'Perhaps one of you could send to the villa for Alice, after all,' she said.

Commander Ricciardi glowered at the party, turned on his heel and strode across the piazza towards the police station. He did not look behind to ensure that Lady Gayle was following.

'Well, really,' she muttered. 'What wonderful manners. Even Constable Ferri was more polite than this.'

When she reached the police station, Commander Ricciardi was standing in the shaded doorway, tapping his stick on the top of his boots.

'You may wait here until your maid arrives if you are too scared to speak to me alone.' He sneered down his long nose at her.

Lady Gayle clenched her fists, digging her nails into the palms of her hand. *Don't let him annoy you. That's exactly what he wants.* 'Thank you, Commander,' she said. 'I shall sit outside here in the sunshine until Alice comes to join me.'

'It is too hot to sit in the sun,' Ricciardi said. 'But it is your choice.' He pushed open the heavy door, allowing it to bang shut behind him and left her outside.

Lady Gayle took a seat on a bench under an olive tree. Judging by the cigarette butts on the floor around the bench, it was a meeting place of sorts—presumably the police officers took their breaks here. Much to her annoyance, however, Ricciardi had been right. It was far too hot to sit in the sun. Lady Gayle wafted her hand in front of her face and hoped that Alice would not take too long.

Across the other side of the square, she watched Charles and Felicity as they stared at her. She shrugged back at them. After a few moments, Felicity strolled across with a waiter immediately behind her. 'We thought you might appreciate a glass of water,' she said, removing a condensation-covered carafe from the tray and placing it and a glass in front of Lady Gayle.

'You are a lifesaver. I didn't want to go into the building alone. But it really is quite hot and sticky out here. He's such a rude man.'

'But very handsome,' said Felicity with a tiny grin.

'He has dead eyes,' retorted Lady Gayle. She rose and drank half the glass of water before waving to Alice, who was hurrying across the piazza, a large bag bouncing on her hip. 'Thank you for the water, Felicity. Now I'd better go and see what this dreadful man wants.'

Lady Gayle twisted the wrought iron handle but still had to put her shoulder to the door to force it open. She stood in the foyer, blinking and allowing her eyes to become used to the low light.

'Where is he?' asked Alice.

'Your guess is as good as mine, I'm afraid. He told me I could wait in here. I'm glad I didn't. I'm already freezing.'

'I did bring a shawl with me in case it was cold inside,' said Alice. She shook the silk shawl out and helped place it around her ladyship's shoulders.

'Thank you, Alice. Shall we see if we can find anyone? Perhaps that desk is a sort of reception?' As she spoke, Constable Ferri appeared via a door hidden in the dark recesses of the foyer. He was weighed down by several manilla folders. 'Constable, could you let Commander Ricciardi know I'm here?'

Constable Ferri glanced in her direction and glowered.

'You must wait. I am not his secretary,' he said. 'The commander will be with you when he is ready.'

Lady Gayle and Alice glanced at each other with raised eyebrows. 'Perhaps we could wait at the café, Alice? It's much warmer there.' As they turned to leave, a shout filled the area.

'Where are you going?' Commander Ricciardi stood in a doorway, his clenched fists on his hips. Behind him, Lady Gayle saw a dimly lit room with a table and four chairs. 'I will speak with you now. You have kept me waiting long enough.'

Lady and maid exchanged a quick glance and strolled towards the commander who, as was his wont, stood tapping his foot.

'Rather impatient, isn't he, milady?' whispered Alice.

Lady Gayle nodded, but all the same, she wandered into the room and took a seat opposite the commander. Alice stood behind her resting her hand on the back of her mistress' chair.

'Why am I here, Commander?' Lady Gayle asked. 'I stated Constable Ferri on the night of the incident.'

'I have questions.' He studied the contents of a folder and then laid it closed on the table. 'Why are you here?'

'You asked me to meet with you, Commander.'

'Don't play games with me. Why are you here in Italy? What is the purpose of your visit?'

'I am convalescing. I have been ill and was told the warmer climate would be beneficial.'

'Why do you stay with Earl Harding?'

'Lord Vickery invited me. He was friends with the Earl and Countess Harding, and he said there was plenty of room.'

'How long have you known Earl Harding?'

'Not long. Only a few days. I met him when I arrived on...' she glanced at Alice. 'Which day was it we arrived?'

'Tuesday, milady,' replied Alice, looking straight ahead and ignoring the militiaman.

Lady Gayle turned to the commander. Head bowed, he was making notes of her answers.

'You are not a business partner of Earl Harding?'

Under the table, Lady Gayle clenched her fists. She shook her head.

'Earl Harding had many English peers invest in his business', said the commander. 'Why didn't you?'

'I suppose because I hadn't heard of it until a short while ago.'

'Do you know people who have invested with him?'

Again, she shook her head.

'Who were the Earl's enemies?'

'How on earth would I know that, Commander Ricciardi? I have been here for around a week or so. Earl Harding spent most of his time ensconced in his study hard at work.'

'He had no liaisons? No secret meetings with a lady?'

'If I had known about any such meetings, they wouldn't be secret, would they? I'm afraid that I am as much in the dark about Earl Harding's death as you are, Commander. I cannot fathom why anyone would want to kill him.'

'Perhaps.' The commander turned to a new page in his notebook. He glanced up at Lady Gayle. 'And Lord Vickery, how long have you known him?'

'Most of my life, Commander.' She sighed with relief at the change in subject. 'Charles is a longtime friend of the family. At one time, he was in the same regiment as my brother.'

'And your brother? He is where?'

'Dead, Commander. Lying in the corner of a foreign field that is forever England, as Mr Rupert Brooke's poem would have it.'

'I see. I am sorry.'

'Thank you. Commander, I have to say, I can't see what my brother or my relationship with Lord Vickery has to do with Earl Harding's death. Could you enlighten me? I was with Miss Makepeace all evening. We returned to the villa at the same time, although Miss Makepeace was a little worse for wear...'

'Worse for wear?'

'She was drunk, Commander. We went to a club, and she had a little too much to drink. When we returned to the villa, Lord Charles and Countess Harding had already returned and were drinking champagne.'

Behind her, Alice coughed.

'Oh, you're quite right, Alice. Countess Harding had spilt champagne on her dress and had gone to her room to change.'

'The countess got her dress wet?'

'Yes, Commander. Soaked with champagne.'

'I see, but you did not see this accident with the champagne. Was it a bottle or simply a glass she spilt?'

'I don't know, Commander. As I have already stated, I was not there and didn't see what happened.'

The commander stared at her for a moment; then he scribbled more notes on his sheet of paper. After a moment, he looked up. 'You and Miss Makepeace got the fountain working, I understand? Before then, it was dry? There was no water?'

'That is correct, Commander.'

'Who's idea was it to get it working?'

'Mine and Miss Makepeace's, as far as I can recall.'

'It was not the idea of Countess Harding?'

'Oh no, Commander, I can't imagine where you got that idea from, but it had nothing to do with the countess.'

CHAPTER THIRTEEN

As Alice and Lady Gayle walked back to the villa, they discussed the curious meeting with the militia commander.

'He asked a lot of questions, milady, but I struggled to understand why he'd asked half of them,' said Alice.

'He was checking our stories against everyone else's. It's exactly what I'd do. Asking about business associates makes sense. If Earl Harding had lost people's money, they would be angry with him. The fountain, though; it was rather odd he asked about that. It's as if he suspects the countess of drowning her husband. That's why I told him her dress was wet from the champagne. I didn't want him jumping to conclusions.'

'She would need to be very strong to force him underwater, milady. The Earl was a large man.'

'Yes, he was, wasn't he?' Lady Gayle tapped her forefinger against her chin. 'Perhaps I should have asked if I could talk to her?'

'Careful, milady.' Alice guided Lady Gayle to the side of the road as the small black car, which they now knew belonged to the police, sped past them towards the villa.

Lady Gayle wafted her shawl in front of her face to disperse the cloud of choking dust.

As the two women walked into the courtyard of Villa Montagna, Countess Beatrice Harding was being gallantly assisted from the back of the car by Constable Ferri.

'Well,' said Alice. 'That's a turn up for the books, isn't it?'

'It is, indeed, Alice. I feel we should welcome the countess home after her trying ordeal.'

However, try as they might, the countess kept to her room and, according to the housemaid, did not want to be disturbed. The poor maid was dispatched to the piazza to fetch meals for the countess, and several bottles of champagne disappeared into the room never to be seen again.

In the middle of the afternoon, Lady Hansen and Teddy Divine sauntered into the courtyard where Lady Gayle, Charles and Felicity loitered, exhausted from the heat.

'Why, y'all look as if you need a break,' drawled Teddy. 'I have just the very thing in mind. There's a casino in the next town. Howzabout we take a trip out there this evening and let our hair down?'

'That's very kind of you Mr Devine,' said Lady Gayle, 'but we couldn't possibly leave Bea here alone while we go out and have fun.'

'Well, I think you should,' insisted Teddy. 'What do you think, Miss Alice?'

Alice, who had just wandered from the kitchen with a tray filled with cold drinks, gave her mistress a puzzled look.

'It's nothing, Alice. Mr Devine wants to take us to a casino this evening, and I said we couldn't possibly leave Countess Harding here on her own.'

'Begging your pardon, milady,' said Alice, 'but I could look after the countess. I could read to her or just sit close by in case she needs anything. I took her a drink just now, but she seems very sleepy.'

'So, that's all settled then,' said Teddy. 'We're all going out. There's a dance floor too if any of you ladies fancy cutting a rug.'

'I really don't think dancing is appropriate, Mr Devine.' Lady Gayle rose to go inside. 'A man has just died, after all. I am shocked that you are not more upset. I hear that the two of you were business partners. That may not have made you friends, but surely you feel something about his passing?' The conversation was over from her point of view.

'Oh, come on, can't you be persuaded, Gigi? I can call you Gigi, can't I?' Teddy Devine grasped her hand, tugging her away from the relief of the villa's cool interior.

'That name, Mr Devine, is reserved for my friends.' Lady Gayle glanced at her hand and then at Teddy's face. He released her hand.

'Well, ain't we all good friends now? Don't tell me you're a sore loser after the treasure hunt last night?'

'I am not a bad loser, Mr Devine. Not when the game is played fair and square. When people cheat? Well, that's an entirely different matter.' She pursed her lips, puzzling over his callous behaviour. *In fact, neither he nor his cousin seemed particularly concerned when we'd just found a dead body. Why is that?*

'I think the casino's a splendid idea,' said Felicity. 'I'm game. What about you, Charles?'

Lord Charles glanced at Lady Gayle. 'It could be just what the doctor ordered, Gigi,' he said. 'If Alice here is prepared to wait on Bea, then I think you should take the opportunity to relax. Have a little flutter, perhaps?'

'What are you all talking about?'

Heads whirled around as Countess Harding strolled into the courtyard. She glanced at the fountain and shuddered before inserting a cigarette into her long, thin holder. She cupped her bony elbow in the opposite hand and tapped her foot in an agitated manner.

'Mr Devine is trying to persuade us to go to a casino with him. Gigi wants to stay and look after you,' replied Charles. He rose and stepped across to the countess and lit her cigarette. 'Her maid Alice has offered to wait on you if you need her.'

'Lady Gayle, if you don't mind me taking advantage of Alice's generosity, I am more than happy for her to stay with me this evening. I agree with Teddy, by way of a change, I think a break would do you all good.'

The drive to the casino that evening took place in silence. I suppose everyone is caught up in their own thoughts about the death of Earl Harding, Lady Gayle surmised. She, too, was thinking over the various options. To hold a man the size of Earl Harding down would have been a hard thing to do. Certainly not something she envisaged Countess Harding being able to achieve—and definitely not without help.

But who would help her? The only people at the villa were Charles and the gardener. Bea was scarcely able to communicate to the gardener about simple things, so Lady Gayle dismissed the idea that she would be able to discuss something as complicated as the murder of her husband. That left Charles. *Poor Charles, why do I always suspect poor Charles?*

She'd had to apologise to him at New Year when she

suspected his involvement in the two deaths which occurred then. *No, I can dismiss Charles from any wrongdoing. I know he's not as pure as the driven snow, but I know he's not a murderer.*

Lady Gayle stared out the car window, watching the countryside fly by. What about people in the other villa, she thought. Not one of them gave the appearance of being saddened by Richard Harding's death. His business partner was taking them all out to a casino to cheer them up, for goodness' sake. It didn't seem right. Utterly heartless.

She opened the window a crack. At least it was cooler now. The day had been quite warm, especially waiting for Alice to accompany her into the police station. She coughed and scrabbled around in her bag for her handkerchief. She laid a hand on her midriff, rubbing the spot where her lungs still rubbed against her ribs. At least the pain isn't as bad; my health must be improving, she thought.

Leaning back in the seat, deciding to think more about the case, Lady Gayle was pulled from her reverie as the car slowed and drew up in front of a magnificent palazzo. Hotel Varelli read the sign overhead.

They had arrived.

CHAPTER FOURTEEN

THE INSIDE OF HOTEL VARELLI WAS AS GLAMOROUS AS ANY OF THE top London hotels. Staff ran over to the new arrivals to relieve them of shawls, scarves, and hats. Then, they were escorted into the dining room for dinner. Teddy Devine was in his element, Lady Gayle noticed. His round face gleamed as the head waiter snapped his fingers, making waiters scurry around at his command.

She caught Count Bianchi's eye, and he gave her a tight smile. 'Americans,' he whispered. 'Always the fuss they must make.'

Lady Gayle dipped her head to hide the grin that his words had caused. However, as her thoughts drifted back to the quiet American man she met in Venice, the smile left her face. No, they were not all brash and belligerent, she thought. *I wonder what he was doing here, and why the gun?*

She nodded at the waiter, who held out her chair for her and placed her bag on the table in front of the dinner setting. Immediately, a glass of champagne appeared within reach, and she took a few sips, relishing the cold liquid against her parched lips. Recalling the day before, she glanced at Felicity who, she saw to her relief, was drinking water.

Eventually, Teddy was satisfied with the arrangements, and as he sat down, waiters began rushing over with the first course. He must have ordered for us all, thought Lady Gayle, but she shrugged, looking at the cold starter of melon and Italian dried ham.

'It's prosciutto. Very tasty.' Charles had leaned over to whisper in her ear. 'It's cured in the mountains. Hung up to dry out over months and months to develop the flavour. Have I got that right, Count Bianchi?'

'Almost, Lord Charles. It is a little more complex. If your ladyship would like to see for yourself, I can arrange a trip to see my small curing operation in the hills nearby.'

Lady Gayle raised her glass to him. 'Thank you, Count Bianchi. That would be very generous of you.'

She gave no indication of whether she would go on such a trip, and she certainly would not go without company. Despite his amusing and wry observations about their American host, his claims to be Richard Harding's friend did not match his behaviour. It left her wary; she did not trust this smooth Italian count.

However, he did not seem to take offence or even notice her lack of agreement. Lady Gayle turned her attention to her food. Charles was right; the flavours of the ham were exquisite, especially when combined with the crispness of the melon. She tucked in and ate as if she'd not eaten in days. When she laid her cutlery on her plate, she looked around at everyone else still eating. She shrugged, thinking that the mountain air must have given her an appetite.

When dinner was over, and it was time to go into the casino, Lady Gayle slowed her pace to match that of Julia Fitzpatrick. The ladies walked side by side without speaking until they were inside the casino area. Before them more people than could have fitted in the dining room spread out in the large gaming room.

Throughout the room, there was a buzz of excitement and anticipation. The clink of glasses battled with the clinking of chips and the rattle of balls as they landed on the roulette wheel. Cheers combined with groans as luck and money changed hands. Elegantly dressed clientele, their jewellery glittering, surrounded every table and waiters rushed around delivering fresh drinks and taking empty glasses away.

As expected, Charles headed for one of the side rooms. Poker, thought Lady Gayle. It really was his game; he never gave anything away with his blank expressions. She thought back to her friends Lord and Lady Ridgewell, with whom she'd stayed at New Year. She fervently hoped Lord Ridgewell was keeping well away from card games. He was never one to keep his thoughts from showing on his face. *I must write to them and see how baby Sylvia is.*

'Shall you play?' Julia Fitzpatrick's words invaded her thoughts, and Lady Gayle turned to face her.

Julia was a handsome woman; one could not say she was beautiful, although her face was not displeasing. It was simply that she wore a constant expression of having caught the smell of something unpleasant—something that displeased her—and made her wrinkle her nose.

'I thought I'd like to watch for a while; perhaps I'll try my hand at something later. I rather fancied blackjack. How about you?'

'I never gamble on anything less than a sure bet,'

replied Julia with a cool smile. She nodded at Count Bianchi, who had taken a place at the roulette wheel.

Is he a sure bet? wondered Lady Gayle, watching the count return the lady's smile. *Is that what she seeks?*

She followed Julia to plush sofas and chairs arranged into an intimate circle at the perimeter of the gaming room. A waiter attired as smartly as any London society butler soon brought cocktails, and they soaked up the atmosphere.

'How long have you known Count Bianchi?' asked Lady Gayle as they had sat in a companionable silence for a while.

'Years, he was friendly with my first husband.'

'You're a widow too?'

Julia gave an enigmatic smile. Lady Gayle took that to mean she was a divorcée. It was always so much easier for the Americans, she thought. English society was so strict about the conventions of marriage—at least on the surface. Beneath the surface, anything goes, she thought, thinking back once more to her New Year break. Not everyone could, or would, divorce so easily.

'Do you think it was a happy marriage?' she found herself asking Julia. 'The Hardings, I mean.'

After exhaling a stream of smoke towards the ceiling, Julia sighed. 'It's hard to say. I think Bea's addiction didn't make her easy to love.'

'Addiction?' murmured Lady Gayle. 'Addicted to what?'

'Snow,' replied Julia. 'That's what has kept her so friendly with your pal Lord Charles all these years.'

Lady Gayle took a large gulp of her cocktail. Cocaine, she thought. She didn't argue with Julia or try to correct her assessment of Charles Vickery. She knew it was true. Charles dabbled in the supply of cocaine to his friends—

she knew about it from personal experience. It had been when she was at her lowest after losing her husband and her baby. She'd needed something to keep her going—not only a reason to get up the following day—but something to block out the pain. However, one day, she woke up. Really woke up to what she was doing to herself. She stopped seeing her London friends and stayed quietly with her parents in Devonshire, fighting her way back to recovery. It had been a long, hard battle, and she often found herself face to face with temptation. She was still winning. So far.

'Do you know how long it's been going on?' She met Julia's dark blue eyes.

Julia shrugged. 'Years. Poor Richard was at his wits' end. He didn't know what to do. He couldn't divorce her. You English are such prudes about divorce, so he was stuck.'

'Countess Harding said they were devoted to each other.'

Silence hung heavy before Julia answered. 'There was devotion...' she said. 'Once. But that was a long time ago. More recently, Bea was devoted to her cocaine, and Richard was devoted to his business, paying for her cocaine and keeping the whole sordid mess quiet from his investors.'

'You seem to know an awful lot about their situation,' said Lady Gayle.

'Yes, I do, don't I?' Julia snatched her cigarette from the end of the holder and stubbed it out in the ashtray. A waiter rushed over with a fresh ashtray and removed the other one. He hovered for a moment, waiting to see if the lady required a light for her next cigarette, but Julia waved him away impatiently. She stared at Lady Gayle for several seconds. Then she blew smoke from her fresh cigarette into the air. 'Richard and I were very close.'

CHAPTER FIFTEEN

Lady Gayle allowed the last comment to hang in the air, not feeling that there was anything she wanted to add out loud. She took a sip of her cocktail, allowing the cool liquid to caress her tongue while her mind raced. Bea had assured her that she and her husband were devoted to each other and, on first meeting them, that was exactly the impression she had gathered for herself. Earl Harding cared deeply for his wife. Lady Gayle was convinced that she hadn't imagined their affection for each other. Or had she? She shook her head. She still felt she wasn't the best judge of character.

In the light of the Harding's mutual affection, Julia's revelation, and her behaviour on seeing Richard's body made no sense. Why wasn't she more upset? However, perhaps that was purely because Julia had redirected her affections to Count Bianchi. After all, the count had no inconvenient wife in the background.

Deciding to question Julia further when they had more privacy, she rose. 'I think I am going to take a stroll around the gaming room. I want to see how the luck of the rest of our party is faring.'

Julia nodded and remained gazing at Count Bianchi. 'Don't do anything I wouldn't do.'

Well, that leaves the field fairly open, doesn't it? There wasn't much, as far as she could see, that the enigmatic American woman wouldn't do. Lady Gayle thought about their strange conversation as she wandered away. Was Julia trying to point the finger of suspicion at Bea? She shook her head as if trying to rid herself of—what? She didn't know what but there was definitely something discomforting about the company of Julia Fitzpatrick. The woman had clearly decided Count Bianchi was going to be her next paramour, if he wasn't already. Lady Gayle found herself almost sympathising with the man despite her own feelings about him.

She gazed around the room, looking for the others in her party. 'Looking for me?' His hot breath on her neck made her shiver despite the warmth of the room.

'Perhaps, I was Charles, and perhaps I wasn't,' she replied. 'However, I was wondering where Felicity had got to.'

'Felicity? Don't tell me you're worried about our little firebrand?'

'I am,' Lady Gayle replied. 'And I'm surprised you're not more worried. I thought you and she were very close once. Wasn't she competing with Lady Sylvia for your hand in marriage not so long ago?'

Charles frowned. 'Where on earth did you get that idea?' He shuffled the chips in his hand. From the colours she could see, Lady Gayle surmised they were all of large denominations.

'Oh, don't tell me,' he said. 'Sylvia told you that Felicity kicked up a fuss when we got engaged?'

Lady Gayle nodded. 'She did happen to mention it.'

'I shouldn't worry about that. It was a bit of a ruse. Felicity pretended to be interested in me so that Sylvia would snap me up.'

'A ruse?' Lady Gayle felt a slight slackening of her facial muscles, and she touched her fingertips to her cheek. 'You mean you used Felicity to encourage Sylvia to accept you? What kind of a rogue are you, Charles?'

'A poor one. Pater isn't always as generous with the allowance as he could be. This helps,' he said, juggling the casino chips in his left hand. 'But a rich wife would have made life a lot easier.'

'I don't know you at all, do I, Charles?' Had he always been so manipulative, she asked herself. And what did that make Felicity? Had she been wrong to place so much trust in her new acquaintance?

He grinned and ran his fingers down her bare arm. 'I've always thought you had the perfect measure of me. You were always my equal in wit and temperament. If you'd had any money when we first met, I would have made you an offer of marriage then.'

'Perhaps it's just as well I didn't have money back then; I don't think we would have been a good match.' Lady Gayle rubbed her arm, trying to erase his touch. 'Now, if you'll excuse me, Charles, I think I'd like to find Felicity. Then I'd like to return to the villa.' Lady Gayle pushed past Lord Charles and dashed through the first door she found.

The room she entered was filled with a sickly-sweet smoke which caught at her throat. Patrons in dinner jackets or haute couture dresses were lying on exquisitely decorated chaises longue. Some of them were being attended to by female servants attired in satin qipao; the high-collared, tight-fitted dress favoured in many Chinese-run establishments. Her attention was drawn to one young woman with dark hair falling around the shoulders of her red satin gown, as she deftly prepared the opium pipe for the man in a dinner jacket. His black tie was undone, and he reclined on the long chair; his eyes rolling back in his head. Lady Gayle waved away a girl dressed in blue. The qipao was embroidered with Chinese dragons and men on horseback. It was beautiful work, and she studied it for a moment before her knees took on a life of their own; she lunged out for something to hold onto before she fell to the floor.

'Lady Gayle, are you quite alright?'

Lady Gayle blinked at the woman before her. 'Miss Blues,' she said, finally recognising the face. 'Are you here to sing?'

Jane Blues laughed, a gentle tinkle like the sound of a brook rushing over stones. 'No, I'm here looking for a friend. He's not an opium addict, but he finds it helps every so often. I wanted to take him home. I didn't realise you partook too.'

'I don't,' replied Lady Gayle. 'Although how long that will be the case if I stay in here any longer, I couldn't say. Have you found your friend?' Staring around the dimly lit room, Lady Gayle struggled to see much through the clouds of thick smoke from the smokers' pipes.

'He's not in here. I've had a good look. Perhaps we need to get you some fresh air?'

'Yes, I'd like that.' Lady Gayle turned around, and Jane Blues opened the door for her. They slipped into the gaming room.

Jane closed the door firmly, but a waft of smoke escaped and hung in the air, resistant to dispersing until a waiter flicked at it with the white cloth he wore over his arm. Jane smiled her thanks at him and led Lady Gayle through the gaming room. Suddenly, she halted, 'What's *he* doing here?' she hissed.

Still suffering the aftereffects of the opium smoke she'd inhaled during her brief sojourn to the smoking room, Lady Gayle took a moment to recover her wits. She shook her head with the hopes of clearing her vision and her thoughts. Then she forced her eyes to follow where Jane was pointing. 'That's Mr Devine,' she said. 'He brought us here this evening. Do you know him too?'

'He's—oh, Oliver, no!' Jane squealed as a tall man rushed over to throw a punch at Teddy Devine.

The punch missed by a mile and Teddy's attacker was wrestled to the floor by three waiters. The man Jane had referred to as Oliver was hauled to his feet and roughly escorted from the gaming room. Teddy Devine merely shrugged and returned to his card game.

'I must go and find him.' Jane ran from the room, and Lady Gayle found herself following.

As they reached the foyer, the three waiters re-entered the building, laughing and dusting off their hands. Jane glowered at them and dashed outside.

Lying on the steps of the hotel was the tall man. He was trying to get up, and Jane urged him to sit while she tended to the cut on his forehead.

'Oliver, what do you think you're playing at?' She dabbed at the cut with a large handkerchief, then opened her handbag and brought out a bottle of disinfectant.

Even in her befuddled state, which was clearing in the warm night air, Lady Gayle was impressed with the foresight Miss Blues demonstrated. Then, it occurred to her that perhaps finding the young man needing medical attention was a frequent event.

'I take it that this is your friend.'

Jane glanced up at her and gave her a quick nod. 'He's not normally like this,' she said.

'I'm going to kill him.' The young man rose to his feet, holding Jane's handkerchief to the cut. 'I mean it, Jane. I'm going to kill him.'

'Please don't say that, Oliver. There has to be a better way.'

'He's ruined me. He and Harding did it deliberately; I know they did.'

'Harding? Do you know Earl Richard Harding?' The words were on Lady Gayle's lips before she could stop herself.

The man glowered at her. 'Yes, I know him. What of it?'

Jane put a restraining hand on the man's chest as he stepped towards Lady Gayle. 'Oliver, don't.'

'Earl Harding is dead,' said Lady Gayle. She was determined to stand her ground and show no fear to this man. 'He was murdered two nights ago.'

'Damnation. I'm too late.' The man spat the words out and staggered away into the night.

Jane called after him, but he didn't respond. 'That's the friend I mentioned the other night. The one that needs help.'

'I surmised as much,' replied Lady Gayle. 'I suppose you had better tell me the rest of the story.'

They turned to go back into the hotel as Charles, Teddy, and the rest of her party began to troop through the front door.

'Oh, there you are, Gigi,' said Charles. 'We were worried

about you. We're heading back now. This place is a bit of a bore after all.'

Lady Gayle turned to look at Jane, who shook her head. She mouthed the word 'later' at Lady Gayle and headed towards her car.

They drove back to the villas in virtual silence. There was no mention of the attack on Teddy. Even Charles kept quiet about his winnings. Felicity could not be drawn on her evening either but did agree to a swim the following day, and Lady Gayle decided to leave any questions until then.

CHAPTER
SIXTEEN

After a subdued breakfast, Felicity and Lady Gayle drove to the mountain lake. It was a relief to get away from the villa and the stifling atmosphere of staffing problems. From the moment she rose, Lady Gayle had dealt with the resignation and immediate departure of Earl Harding's valet, the gardener claimed someone had stolen his hat and jacket, and the housemaid declared the villa was full of ghosts. Only Alice remained her usual stoic and steadfast self.

They swam in the chilly water, after which they rubbed their skin briskly with towels to restore some heat in to their bodies. They devoured much of the picnic that Alice had prepared for them in very short order. Replete and happy, Lady Gayle lay back on her towel, feeling the sun on her face and warming her skin. The cough had finally subsided, she realised, and she was well on the road to recovery. It was not before time.

She sat up and, resting her forearms on her knees, Lady Gayle stared out over the water. It was now or never. 'Do you still love Charles?'

'Me? No. What on earth gave you that idea? I think he's more interested in you.'

'What about last year? Weren't you madly in love with him then?'

Felicity sat up. 'You've got no reason to be jealous, Gigi. I don't love Charles, and I never have done. He's always been like my big brother. I'm sure if you give him time to recover from Lady Sylvia's death, he'll come around to your charms. In all honesty, I think he already has.'

Lady Gayle shot to her feet. She ran to the water's edge and began wading into the cold lake. How could she have been such a fool? Charles had lied to her. He'd lied to Sylvia. She was an idiot to have trusted him. She struck out into the deeper waters of the lake, feeling the chilly waves wash over her. She plunged down to the pebbles at the bottom and snatched a couple of them. Lungs bursting, she kicked her way to the surface, where she threw the stones away as far as she could. Twisting in the water, she saw Felicity standing on the shoreline. I should have trusted her all along, she thought.

Putting her face in the water, Lady Gayle swam back to the beach, full of a new resolve to discover who was responsible for Earl Harding's death.

'Your friend Miss Blues was at the casino last night. Did you see her?' Lady Gayle towelled herself dry again and dressed.

'Only at a distance,' replied Felicity. 'She was driving away when I came out the casino. I didn't know she was contracted to sing there too.'

'She wasn't singing. She had been looking for her friend. The one who was swindled.'

'Ah, him,' said Felicity. She sat on the small beach, idly throwing pebbles into the water.

Lady Gayle ate some grapes whilst waiting for Felicity to tell all she knew. She didn't have to wait long.

'He's called Oliver, Oliver Thornton. I know he was absolutely beastly to Uncle Richard. Tried to take him to court over money.'

'Do you know why exactly?'

Felicity shook her head. 'No, not back then. I didn't believe it at the time. Then I came out here and met Janey. I heard the other side of the story. That's when I heard just how utterly vile Uncle Richard could be. He and Teddy Devine set Oliver up—I overheard Teddy talking to Uncle Richard, he said, "We'll get the sucker to take the fall." I didn't know what that meant at the time, but they got Oliver on the board of some company or other. Made him a director, and when it went bust, all the liability was Oliver's.'

'Was this the Imperial Ventures Group?'

'Yes.' Felicity whispered so quietly. Lady Gayle had to edge closer to her to hear. 'I had heard of it when Charles mentioned it, but I didn't want either of you to know. I thought you might think I was involved somehow.'

'And well I might,' said Lady Gayle. 'Although it would have been nice to have made the assessment on my own. You can trust me, you know that, don't you, Felicity.'

'I suppose so.'

'Well, I think we'd better be getting back to the villa; we can't leave your Aunt Bea alone all day.'

'She's not my aunt. As I told you, Richard was more of a guardian than my uncle. He had control of my money. I suppose he doesn't any longer, does he?'

Felicity turned to Lady Gayle. Her face split with a huge grin as the realisation struck her.

Lady Gayle raised her eyebrows. 'It's a jolly good job I know you can't have killed him, as you were with me all the time.'

'Oh yes, you're my alibi, aren't you?' Felicity rose and hauled Lady Gayle to her feet. 'I suppose we'd better get back. See what the commander has found out in our absence.'

After packing up their picnic things, they trudged to the car, neither keen to return to the villa and the commander's investigations.

Felicity started the engine and put the car in gear. As she pulled away, Lady Gayle glanced at her, wondering what she knew about Bea Harding's addiction to cocaine. Although she didn't trust her own instincts about Julia Fitzpatrick, she knew the woman was telling the truth about this. She'd seen enough evidence of the drug's effects for herself with Bea's mood swings and skeletal appearance. It was a stark reminder of her own life and appearance only a few short years ago.

The powerful car roared down the mountainside, and Lady Gayle clung to her cloche hat as her heart pulsated in time with the motor. Despite all the chaos and concerns which awaited them at the villa, she was still glad she'd visited this part of Italy. Dr Sloane had been right; the warm weather was doing her recovery the world of good.

She was gazing into the valley, watching the tops of the tall cypress trees which surrounded farmhouses and villas swaying in the breeze, when she heard Felicity's yell over the sound of the engine. Snatched from her reverie, she clutched the handle on the car door. The car slewed across the road, the tyres squealing in protest. Her body was slammed firstly into the car door, then thrown across the seats to collide with Felicity. She braced herself, trying desperately to allow the younger woman to battle with the spinning car. Gripping the edge of her seat, Lady Gayle hoped she would not be flung from the car onto the hard road. Finally, the spinning stopped, and the car screeched to a halt on a grassy verge. Shaking, she glanced down the vertiginous slope into the valley below, which was now only a few inches from her door.

Felicity was hanging onto the steering wheel, breathing heavily. She peeked over the top of the steering wheel to stare at the cause of their swerve. On its side ahead of them was a black car and beside it a small donkey cart which Felicity had narrowly missed. The driver of the black car had been thrown from their vehicle. Their body lay like a discarded toy in a crumpled heap against the base of a wall, which remained from when the road had been carved from the mountainside.

Lady Gayle scrambled over into the back seat and out of the Bugatti to tend to the wounded driver. The driver of the donkey cart was wailing but seemed unhurt. As she approached, Lady Gayle scented the metallic tang of the blood which covered the man's head. She half turned but kept pushing herself towards him—after all, she told herself, he *could* still be alive. Although she knew it was hopeless, she knelt by the man. That's when she saw his pale face. She touched her fingertips to close his blank eyes, which still seemed to stare at the infinite blue sky above.

It was Teddy Devine, and he was dead.

CHAPTER SEVENTEEN

Lady Gayle rocked back on her heels. Hearing a gasp beside her, she realised that Felicity had followed her lead. Clearly, the younger woman had left her car and decided to take a look too.

'That's Teddy's car,' she murmured. 'Is that him? Is he dead?'

Lady Gayle rose and clasped Felicity by her shoulders. She pulled the young woman in close for a hug. 'Yes, he's dead, and you need to drive down into the village and get help. Can you do that?'

Felicity nodded. She squared her jaw and nodded once more. Dashing back to her car, she leapt in, eased the car around the crash site and sped off down the hillside in the direction of the village.

Lady Gayle smiled after her realising that, in avoiding the crash site and her car careening down the hill, she'd had a glimpse of what made the young woman such a formidable racing driver.

Turning to the driver of the donkey cart, Lady Gayle felt at a loss. Despite his confusion, the old man and his beast seemed unhurt. She ran her hands over the small animal's spine, down his front and back legs to make sure nothing was broken, but the little creature appeared to be fine. He nuzzled at her, and she scratched him behind his enormous ears.

The old man kept muttering something that she was unable to make out, other than the word *macchina*. She presumed that he was complaining about how fast the visitors drove on these small mountainous roads. She couldn't blame him. She offered him some wine from the picnic basket that Alice had packed, but he shook his head and pulled out a wineskin from under a blanket in his cart. They sat on the side of the road together, with the old man muttering away to himself and drinking from his wine skin.

It seemed like she sat for hours on the side of the road. The old man was quieter now, and Lady Gayle glanced at him to make sure he was well. Her mind flashed back to the Western Front and the grey faces of soldiers suffering from shellshock. She remembered one of her "sitters", not ill enough to need a stretcher, the young man rocked himself back and forth for comfort. She thought he would recover fully and was devastated to hear that he'd died a few days later. It was the first time she'd known someone die from shock.

She shook her head to clear her mind of the past and felt the old man's pulse. It was normal. He would be fine, she realised with relief. She wandered over to look at Teddy—the once vibrant young man was now a mere shell. It was a grim reminder that death was always close at hand. 'Did you kill Earl Harding, Teddy?' she whispered.

He didn't reply, and although she'd closed his eyes, she

wished she had something to cover his face. She berated herself, knowing she should have taken one of the swim towels from Felicity's car.

Eventually, the roar of the Bugatti could be heard making its way up the mountainside. Charles leapt out of the vehicle and was beside her. Alice was there too and threw a shawl around her shoulders.

'I've made you some sweet tea for the shock, milady,' she said.

'I'm fine, thank you, Alice.' She squeezed Alice's hand. Clearly, she wasn't the only one today using their skills gained in wartime. Alice had been a nursing auxiliary when they'd met. 'I don't think I'm in shock. Obviously, I am dreadfully shaken to see Teddy dead like that, but I feel fine.'

'What on earth happened?' Charles was on his knees in front of her. 'Did you hit him or something?'

'No, of course not. We would have collided with Teddy's car if Felicity wasn't such a terrific driver. She swerved, and we were fine. The accident had already happened when we arrived. I suppose he must have tried to avoid hitting the old man and his cart and hit the bank instead.'

Charles nodded and went to speak to the old man. Lady Gayle looked over at them. She didn't know Charles spoke Italian, but then she was finding out there was quite a lot she didn't know about Viscount Charles Vickery.

When Charles returned, his face was grave. He knelt down once more. 'The old man says there was another car. He says the other car tried to drive Teddy's off the road.'

'Is he sure?'

'He's sure. As he told me, he's old, not daft. He doesn't know what type of car it was, just black.' Charles rose at the sound of a car engine. Lady Gayle was braced for another accident, but the driver slowed the vehicle as if they were prepared for what they would find. They were.

The driver in police uniform leapt out the car and strode smartly to the rear door, which he opened. Commander Ricciardi had arrived.

The militia man unfurled himself from the rear seat. Again, Charles took charge and spoke to the police officer. Lady Gayle stood. She was beginning to get a little annoyed at Charles taking over, but Commander Ricciardi was not like Constable Ferri—he wanted to talk to the eyewitnesses, all of the witnesses, regardless of their gender.

Unlike Detective Inspector Coward, who she knew would ask after her health, Commander Ricciardi jumped straight into questions.

After hearing everything she had related to Charles, Commander Ricciardi questioned Felicity. He was quite voluble, and Lady Gayle was on the point of remonstrating with him when another car arrived.

'What on earth is he doing here?'

'Who?' said Charles, turning to follow her gaze. 'Oh, him,' was all he said as the Pinkerton detective approached Commander Ricciardi.

The two men spoke in hushed but rapid Italian. Their constant glances at Charles and Lady Gayle as they talked made the pair realise that they were the topic of conversation.

When Alex Cornwall strolled over to speak to them, Lady Gayle held out her hand. 'How lovely to see you again, Mr—'

'Martins. Danny Martins,' Alex Cornwall said quickly. 'I'm a Pinkerton detective.' He showed his badge to them both.

'How can we help you, detective?' said Charles.

Lady Gayle hadn't failed to notice that Charles had edged forward, his left shoulder placing a blockage between her and the Pinkerton man. She frowned up at him, an expression that only Mr Cornwall, or was it really Martins, noticed.

Mr Martins grinned at Lady Gayle, and Lord Charles clenched his fists. 'What is a Pinkerton doing here?' Lord Charles growled. 'Aren't you a little out of your jurisdiction, Mr Martins?'

'As long as I'm fighting for justice, nowhere is out of my jurisdiction, Lord Charles. Although that,' he pointed at Teddy Devine's body, 'does tend to mess with my purview.'

'What business did you have with Mr Devine?' asked Lady Gayle.

'It's nothing to do with us, Gigi,' Charles said in a low voice. 'All I can tell you, Mr Martins, is that Teddy Devine was a new acquaintance. We hardly knew him.' He clasped his hand on Lady Gayle's elbow and guided her towards the Bugatti.

When she tried to pull away, he hissed in her ear. 'I don't trust that man one bit. We need to leave, and we need to do that now. Please, Gigi, for once in your life, will you listen to me and do as I ask?'

Reluctantly, Lady Gayle demurred, although she did wrench her elbow from Charles' grasp. She glared at him, 'This isn't over,' she said.

CHAPTER EIGHTEEN

Although Charles hadn't exactly lied to the Pinkerton detective, Lady Gayle was uncomfortable with how the conversation had been left. She slipped onto the back seat of the Bugatti—Charles was in the front with Felicity—and she gazed out the window as they drove slowly back to the villa.

Her mind raced. Whilst she had not known Teddy Devine at all well, others did; she'd also learned a great deal from reading Mr Conan Doyle's Sherlock Holmes novels. For example, she knew that to find out *why* someone was killed, it was best to learn as much as possible about the person and how they had lived. If what the old cart driver had told Charles was true, then someone had deliberately tried to drive Teddy Devine and his car off the road. After his declaration last night, the only person she could think of was Oliver Thornton. All she had to do now was find out where he lived.

'Felicity, would you mind awfully dropping me in the piazza rather than at the villa?' She leaned forward and spoke as loudly as she could over the sound of the throaty engine.

Charles twisted in his seat. 'I thought we agreed no more detecting. I told you that Pinkerton is dangerous.'

Lady Gayle smiled as sweetly as she could. She was right; she *had* sensed tension between the men. All the same, she could not understand how Charles knew the detective. 'We agreed nothing of the sort, Charles. However, I simply want to pay a call on someone. Nothing to worry yourself about.'

Felicity called over her shoulder. 'We'll drop Charles off at the villa, and I'll come with you. I'd like to see Jane too.'

Charles glowered at them both and folded his arms. He faced the windscreen and stared out at the road ahead, occasionally pointing out to Felicity twists and obstacles in the road. Felicity bore it all with a blank expression on her face. Her tightened jaw, however, told a different story. When she pulled into the driveway for the villa, Charles exited the car reluctantly. By way of a change, how he felt about the situation was written all over his face. He was not impressed.

With a cheery wave, Felicity gave Lady Gayle enough time to jump into the passenger seat, and they drove towards the centre of the small town.

'Jane will most likely be at home,' shouted Felicity over the roar of the engine. 'Fortunately, I know exactly where that is.'

Lady Gayle nodded, hoping that the man who'd grabbed and argued with Jane on the night they had been introduced to the singer at the nightclub would not be there. She had no idea who he was, nor his connection to Jane, but she knew a wrong'un when she saw one.

Felicity pulled into a side street and parked. 'It's up

there,' she said, pointing to a flat above the bakery shop.

Lady Gayle looked up, pleased to see that the windows were open, a good sign that their quarry was at home. Hopefully, Jane would be in a chatty mood.

Felicity pushed at a front door located between two shops, and Lady Gayle followed her up the narrow stairway. With each step, she wondered if they would be bringing news to Jane or simply reiterating information that she already had. One glance at the singer's face when she opened the door to them said it all. She knew exactly why they were there.

'Is Oliver here?' said Lady Gayle as she was invited into the flat.

Jane shook her head. 'I haven't seen him since last night.'

'But you know what's happened, don't you? You know why we are here. I can see it in your face.' Lady Gayle looked around the sitting room while she waited for an answer. It was much more spacious than she'd imagined it to be and was beautifully appointed with charming ornaments and paintings.

'We know.'

Lady Gayle whirled around to face the owner of the gruff voice. It was the thug from the nightclub. 'May I confirm what it is you know? And how?'

'We were in the café when Felicity came to the police station. The commander was in the café too. We heard her say there'd been an accident and that it was Teddy who'd been killed.'

Lady Gayle raised her eyebrows at Felicity, who at least had the grace to look embarrassed. She'd have to speak to her later about the importance of discretion in detection work later, but for now, the moment of surprise was lost.

Jane and her thug had had plenty of time to prepare a story if that was what they needed to do. She sighed.

'What do you know about Teddy?' she said, lowering herself onto the sofa. She suddenly felt very weary.

'I think you mean Theodore Devine the third,' laughed the thug. 'He's bad news, especially if you have any money. Like his father in that respect. There's nothing Teddy likes more than parting people from their money. Isn't that right, Janie?'

Jane nodded and flopped into a basketweave chair by the open window. 'His father's a banker in New York, but there are rumours, just rumours, you understand, that the father's crooked too.'

'In what way?' asked Lady Gayle, 'and what has any of this got to do with Oliver...'

'The family name is Thornton,' said Jane. 'But he's also Viscount Etherington.'

Lady Gayle closed her eyes and let out a deep sigh. *That's why the name was familiar when Felicity mentioned it.* She knew the story. Or at least she knew some of it. The son had lost the entire family fortune, and Lord Etherington had been forced to sell the family estate, which had been in the family for generations. His lordship currently lived on the generosity of friends. What had become of the son, she knew not. Or at least, not until now.

'Small world, isn't it?' said Jane. 'Oliver landed up here a few months ago to work in a vineyard. I believe it belongs to a family friend who was prepared to give him a home and teach him how to make wine.'

The thug guffawed, and Lady Gayle regarded him with a cold stare.

'Oliver is better at drinking the wine than making it,' said the man with a shrug. 'What can I say? He's a loser—'

'Ignore my brother. It's not Olly's fault.' Jane jumped from her chair, stepping towards the thug, who unexpectedly flinched.

'I'm just saying,' he growled.

'Well, you're not telling it right. Oliver was duped by Teddy Devine and Earl Harding. They played him and reeled him in like a fish.'

'I think you'd better tell me the whole story,' said Lady Gayle. She looked from Jane to the thug she was claiming as her brother and wondered if they were truly siblings or not.

'It's probably better coming from me.' The bedroom door creaked open, and Oliver Thornton, dressed in the clothes he'd worn the night before, stood in the doorway.

He strolled into the room and kissed Jane chastely on the cheek. 'Thanks for protecting me, both of you,' he said. He sat in the chair Jane had recently vacated and began his tale.

Much of the story Lady Gayle already knew from following it in the newspapers, but all the same she listened quietly for those snippets the papers had not included.

'Harding first approached my father, Lord Etherington, but when Pops turned him down, he came to me. Said my father was an old stick in the mud, that Imperial Ventures needed young blood and ambition. He used all the right words to entice me, and enticed I was. Once I was hooked and heavily invested, I met Theodore Devine III. You know him as Teddy. I knew at once I'd made a mistake, and I tried to cash in my shares. Teddy explained to me why that was a mistake.

'Earl Harding had convinced me to become a director of the company. At first, I objected because Imperial Ventures wasn't a limited liability company.' Oliver paused to ensure his audience understood the relevance.

Felicity gave the merest of shrugs, and Oliver nodded.

'If a company is limited liability, and it goes broke, the creditors can't take the owners' cash and property to repay the debts. Teddy, I discovered, had forged the indemnity papers. I became a director. I didn't realise until later that I was the sole director.

'How much later?' murmured Lady Gayle.

'When the bailiffs came knocking on my door,' replied Oliver with a sheepish grin. 'I jumped out the window and shimmied down the drainpipe.'

'Your father, an elderly man, lost everything,' said Lady Gayle. 'I don't suppose he could have escaped via a drain-pipe even if one had been conveniently at hand. He was lucky he was spared prison.'

'It wasn't my fault,' said Oliver.

'So, you say. Tell me, where does the Pinkerton come in? What does he want?'

Oliver's knuckles covering the end of the chair's arms whitened. 'He was after Devine. It was nothing to do with me. I was just one of many people tricked by Teddy. I—'

Whatever more he had planned to say was drowned out by the battering of fists on the street door at the bottom of the narrow stairs.

Oliver started. He jumped up, looking around like a rat in a trap. Then he dashed back into the bedroom and jumped over the balcony. Lady Gayle darted after him. She leaned over the balcony railings to see Oliver Thornton waving as he drove off in a small black car.

His cheerful wave, in such contrast to his earlier actions, only raised Lady Gayle's suspicions about Viscount Etherington further.

CHAPTER NINETEEN

Lady Gayle found herself roughly thrust aside as Commander Ricciardi dashed onto the balcony to shake his fist at the departing motorist. She pushed past him back into the bedroom and returned to Jane's sitting room.

Constable Ferri stood smirking in the doorway he was blocking. Whilst he was not tall, he was wide enough to prevent anyone leaving the flat by the stairs.

Deciding that he would not prevent her from leaving, Lady Gayle collected her small handbag from the floor by the chair where she had been sitting. 'Come along, Felicity,' she said. 'We are not needed here.' She strode to the doorway and narrowed her eyes at the constable. For a moment, it seemed that he would stand his ground, but as she stepped closer, he suddenly recoiled as if she had slapped him. She bit back her sigh of relief, refusing to let the constable see that deep down, she was a little intimidated. She hated bullies.

'Felicity,' she called over her shoulder. 'We're leaving. There's nothing more we can do. I am sorry, Jane. Hopefully, Viscount Etherington will see sense and hand himself in.'

As she reached the bottom step, a man blocked her exit to the street. 'Please excuse me, Mr Martins, or Cornwall or whatever your name is. I have somewhere I need to be.'

With a smile, the detective lifted his trilby and stepped to one side. 'Could you tell Sir Charles that I'll be dropping by later?'

Lady Gayle sighed. 'His title is either Viscount Vickery or Lord Charles. He's a peer of the realm, not a knight. His names are not difficult to grasp, unlike your own.'

'My apologies. But tell him all the same, won't you?'

With a deep breath, Lady Gayle was on the point of saying something quite rude, but she remembered her manners in time and strode away. Without the heft of the bustle that her Mama still wore under her dresses on occasion, she felt that her exit lacked some dignity, but all the same, it felt good. She was sure Mama would have been proud.

'Do you want me to go after him?' A broad grin across her face, Felicity held her right hand over her eyes, shielding them from the sun. 'Bugle can catch him.'

Bugle? wondered Lady Gayle, she'd not heard Felicity call the Bugatti by a name before, but of course, it suited the car. Well, almost.

'I think he's got too much of a head start on us, and in any case, do you know where he was going?'

'To the vineyard?' Felicity suggested, but as she spoke, the clanging of the police cars' klaxons could be heard as they raced out of the town.

'I think the commander has beaten us to it,' replied Lady Gayle. 'However, I believe this case needs brainpower, not racing around like mad things after suspects.'

'If you say so.' With her shoulders sagging, Felicity dropped into the driver's seat and started the engine.

Lady Gayle got in beside her, and they went back to Villa Montagna Verde.

On returning to the villa, Lady Gayle retired to her room to freshen up. She rapidly ate the sandwiches that Alice had prepared for her, grateful once again for her maid's foresight.

'How has the countess been this morning, Alice?' she asked as she slipped a pale green frock over her head. She admired the handkerchief-style hem in the mirror, twirling around to show it to greater effect.

Alice didn't answer immediately, and Lady Gayle turned her attention from the dress to her maid. 'Alice?' she said. 'Is there something wrong?'

Alice pursed her lips before speaking, a sure sign that she wasn't sure how what she had to say would be met.

'Tell me,' Lady Gayle prompted. She perched on the end of the bed and patted the spot beside her.

Reluctantly, Alice sat down next to her mistress. 'She's very up and down, milady,' said Alice, twisting her hands in her lap. 'One minute she's in floods of tears, and the next she's bursting with energy. I don't understand it.'

'I do,' said Lady Gayle. 'Has Lord Charles been to see her?'

'He sat with her in the courtyard when he came back. I suppose he wanted to tell her about the accident.'

'How did she take the news?'

'She was upset at first, and then she cheered up. I think Lord Charles gave her something. I saw him holding her hands, which I thought was a little odd, but of course, he could have been comforting her. She had been crying, and this death has been yet another shock for her.'

'What happened next, Alice? Did you see?'

'Oh, yes, milady. I thought, as you would want to know everything, so I remained by the window, hidden by the muslin.'

'Oh, well done, Alice. Absolutely topping spy work.'

Alice giggled and dipped her head. Her cheeks flushed as they always did when she was complimented. 'I heard Lord Charles say he'd get some more champagne, and he left her in the courtyard. As soon as he went, Countess Harding opened a tiny vial and tipped the contents into a tea plate. It looked like a white powder. She used a bank note to sniff it up her nose. She popped the vial into one of the plant pots, milady.'

Lady Gayle nodded. She had a good idea what had been in the vial, but in any case, she'd go and find the evidence. 'Go on,' she said.

'Well, then Lord Charles came back, and he poured her some fresh champagne. The countess took a sip, and she seemed to brighten right up. Much happier she was. Wiped her tears dry and danced around the courtyard with Lord Charles, laughing her head off.'

'How did Lord Charles react?'

'Oh, he was laughing too, milady. Very happy they both looked.'

Lady Gayle rose and looked out the window onto the courtyard. Bea Harding was no longer out there, but the chair where she had been sitting was still there; an upturned bottle of champagne was sitting in an ice bucket.

'Alice, was the countess in the courtyard all morning?'

'I couldn't say, milady. I had my duties to attend to in here and I went to the shops to fetch things for your sandwiches. You have to be so careful with the timings here. The shops aren't open all day, such as they are back home.'

'Quite,' Lady Gayle murmured. 'Siesta time. Everything shuts up for the hottest part of the day.' She stood by the window, lost in thought. Her mind raced. She needed to check the vial to be certain. Nibbling the last sandwich, she made up her mind.

'I'm going to see if I can find the vial.'

'Should I come with you, milady?'

'No, keep watch from up here. I won't be long.' She tiptoed down the stairs and peeked into the courtyard. No one was in sight, but now siesta was almost over, someone might reappear at any moment. She strolled over to the abandoned chairs and peered into the large terracotta pot. The tiny vial was there at the base, smashed into minuscule pieces. 'Blast,' she muttered.

At the sound of footsteps behind her, she whirled around. The housemaid was approaching. Undoubtedly intent on tidying up the mess Bea had left behind. Lady Gayle saw the tea plate lurking under the sunchair. She snatched it up and placed her finger over the minute grains she saw there. Hiding her hand behind her back, she allowed the housemaid to collect the plate and the glasses. When the girl returned to the villa, she looked at her fingertip and the few grains that were still adhered. She stuck out her tongue and tasted the powder. Her mind flooded with memories, and she spat the grains into a handkerchief. She didn't want to be tempted again.

However, it was clear Charles was up to his old tricks, and he was supplying snow to the countess. Although where he had sourced, it was anyone's guess. Nonetheless, it would appear that Julia Fitzpatrick had told the truth.

Bea Harding was a cocaine addict. It only left one question. What else had Julia told the truth about?

CHAPTER TWENTY

Lady Gayle ran back to her bedroom. She was on the point of revealing everything she'd just discovered to Alice when her maid stepped smartly to the bedroom door to answer it. Lady Gayle turned around in surprise. Over the pounding of her breath, the quiet knock had not reached her ears.

Felicity Makepeace stood in the doorway. 'Are we going to go over the suspects?' she said, glancing at Alice. 'That's what you sleuths do next, isn't it? Oliver must be at the top of the list after running off like that.'

Lady Gayle raised her eyebrows at Alice, who took the notebook and pen from the drawer; she placed them in her ladyship's hand.

'Shall I make some tea, milady?'

'I think champagne is a much better idea,' said Felicity.

'Tea,' said Lady Gayle firmly. 'Alice is quite right. Tea would be much better. We need to keep clear heads. Don't worry, Alice, we won't start without you. I'll tell Felicity everything you've just told me.'

Alice bobbed a curtsy and left, returning promptly with tea, biscuits, and sandwiches.

If Felicity noticed the third cup and saucer on the tray, she said nothing.

'Very well,' said Lady Gayle, taking a cup of tea from Alice. 'We know from the old man with the donkey that a car tried to drive Mr Devine off the road. So, from that, I think we can conclude that his death was not an accident. However, I do believe that *making* it look like an accident was intentional.'

'You do?' said Felicity. 'Why would someone want to do that? I thought we all agreed that the murders are connected?'

'We do, yes. I certainly believe there's a connection, but I think by making the other death look like an accident, I feel the killer hoped it would throw the investigators off the scent.'

'Very foolish of them, in that case, milady,' said Alice.

'Thank you, Alice.'

'And the connection is the Imperial Ventures Group?' Felicity took a sip of her tea and frowned. 'I do wish we were having champagne. We're solving a murder, two murders, in fact. That absolutely feels like a champagne moment.'

'Champagne when we've solved it,' said Lady Gayle. 'Clear heads in the meantime. Now, who do we know who had been ruined by the Imperial Ventures Group?'

'Charles and Oliver,' announced Felicity. 'Oliver admitted he'd been ruined, and he ran away while we were questioning him.'

'He ran away when the commander arrived,' said Lady Gayle. 'Not from us, remember. He seemed happy to talk to us. He has good reason to fear the police, and since he drove off in a car similar to that seen by the old man, he's put himself even more at risk. Tell me, Felicity, why do you suspect Charles? He didn't lose money with Imperial Ventures. He told us he didn't. If he had, would he remain on friendly terms with your uncle?'

'They argued before you arrived. You should have heard them. A right old ding dong it was.'

'They? Oliver and Charles argued? I didn't realise they knew each other.'

'No. Uncle Richard and Charles argued.'

'Are you sure it was about the company?' Lady Gayle knew that there was a much greater reason for the men to argue than over Imperial Ventures.

Felicity shrugged. 'I'm not sure. What else would it be about?'

Lady Gayle exchanged a quick look with Alice and shook her head as if to say she had not told the girl Lord Charles was supplying the countess with drugs.

'Do you have any other suspects in mind?' Felicity spoke softly, twisting her teacup on its saucer.

'I might, but I have to ask you some questions about your aunt.'

'She's not my aunt,' muttered Felicity.

'That's by the by. What can you tell me about her? She and your uncle never had children?'

'No, she couldn't, apparently. I don't know the ins and outs. Well, I wouldn't, would I? They still think *I'm* a child.'

'But they weren't troubled by it?'

Felicity shrugged. 'I think Uncle Richard would have liked a son, but they got on tolerably well, considering.'

'Considering?'

'Beatrice has mood swings. They've become worse over the last couple of years. Sometimes, she's fine, and sometimes she's a monster. I tend to make myself scarce on those occasions.'

Lady Gayle nodded. 'How long have these mood swings been going on?'

'Like I said, a couple of years, more or less. Look, we know she can't have run Teddy off the road; she can't drive. If you think there are other suspects, shouldn't we be talking about them?'

'Yes, of course, I have a few people in mind. Although, other than Oliver, I cannot think of anyone who would want them both dead.'

'Is there anyone you don't suspect? What about me?'

'You were with me. Both times, as it happens. I am quite happy that you are not involved. Other people might want Earl Harding dead, but not Mr Devine and vice versa.'

'So, you don't suspect me, and you don't suspect Charles, then who *is* on your list?'

'Count Bianchi. I know Charles said he hadn't invested with Imperial Ventures, but we don't know that for certain. Then there is your singer friend, Miss Blues. Are she and Oliver only friends? She was very angry on his behalf.'

'Jane wouldn't do anything like that! She's too gentle.'

'Yet, I saw her as we were leaving the nightclub on the night of the treasure hunt. She was keeping to the shadows and definitely didn't want to be seen. And what's the story with that brute of a man? I saw him threaten her when we were at the club.'

'He's her brother and her manager. He gets a bit over-protective, but he's fine,' said Felicity. 'What about Julia Fitzpatrick? I know she hated Uncle Richard.'

Lady Gayle coughed, and Alice looked at her with concern. She shook her head as if to say her cough wasn't important just now. 'Why do you think Julia hated your uncle? Have you seen them argue?'

'No. It's just an impression I have. She's always glaring at him when I can see he's done nothing wrong.'

'What reason would she have to kill her cousin, though? If we agree that the two deaths are connected.' Lady Gayle's mind raced. Rather than finding out what Julia Fitzpatrick had been honest about, she was uncovering a lie. She needed to talk to the American divorcée immediately. She glanced at her watch. It was getting late, almost time for dinner. Perhaps she could talk with Julia at the restaurant —if they could get some time alone together.

'This isn't easy, is it?' Felicity rose. 'What do you do next?'

'I note down all my suspects,' said Lady Gayle with a smile, 'and then I question them. I find out their reasons and their alibis. I write all that down, and I think about what doesn't add up.'

'It all sounds terribly dull,' replied Felicity. 'It's always much more exciting in the detective stories.'

'It's not all chasing around and looking for clues, Felicity,' said Lady Gayle. 'Sometimes the truth is right in front of you. All you have to do is stop for a moment, take in your surroundings, and see the situation for what it is.'

CHAPTER TWENTY-ONE

'So, come on. Tell me, who's first on *your* list?' insisted Felicity. 'Charles, I presume, since we don't know where Oliver ran off to.'

'Where is this vineyard that Oliver was working at?' Lady Gayle firstly tapped her pen on her notebook and then against her chin.

'Do you think he would run to his lair like that?' Felicity seemed puzzled by the question. 'Surely he'd try to get away properly. Especially if he thinks the police are after him?'

'I think he'd go where he felt safe.'

'Who was he living with?' said Alice. 'Miss Felicity said beforehand Mr Oliver had come to stay with friends. That they took him in when he ran away before.'

Lady Gayle nodded. Not only was Alice right about that, but she made another valid point, whether she knew it or not.

'Good thinking, Alice. Oliver runs away. Whenever there's trouble, he takes to his heels. In fact, the only time he's been active was when he thumped Teddy at the casino.

Previously, when the authorities have come after him, he's done a runner. From England and again today from Jane's flat. That's not the action of a killer, is it?' Lady Gayle looked at the two women. They both shook their heads, but she thought even if Oliver wasn't a killer by nature, it didn't mean he hadn't become one. Both murders could have been done in a fit of rage. Drowning someone. Driving someone off the road. Those were actions that could have been planned out ahead of time but equally could have been carried out without any thought at all.

'Felicity, do you know where Oliver was working? Who was this friend who took him in? Any ideas?'

Felicity laid her teacup on the dresser and crossed to stare out the window. 'I've been giving it some thought, and I think it was Count Bianchi,' she said. 'He's a big landowner, and, as you've already seen, he has a number of properties and enterprises.'

'Let's go and have an early dinner; if we're lucky, we can talk to the count.' Lady Gayle rose and smoothed out her dress. She glanced at Alice. 'Will you keep an eye on Countess Harding again? I am still worried about her.' Lady Gayle touched her finger to her nose, and Alice nodded. She knew her maid would understand the signal without letting on to Felicity that her aunt, by marriage, was a drug addict. As for Bea's cocaine supplier... well, she would deal with Charles later.

Unfortunately, none of the people they wanted to talk to made it to dinner. So, the following morning, Felicity and Lady Gayle had no choice but to pay Count Bianchi and Julia Fitzpatrick an uninvited visit.

Unlike the Villa Montagna Verde, Villa Colli di Firenze

was painted in white, surrounded by formal gardens and intricate water works. Small channels allowed water to flow from one section to another. It was serene and picturesque, with neatly trimmed hedges and symmetrical flower beds with ornate floral displays. It was the quiet, understated wealth of old money and Lady Gayle found herself admiring the glamour and precise planning which had created the vision before her. She snapped her mind away from wondering if she could incorporate such gardens into the grounds of Bethencourt Castle and marched to the front door.

'I will ascertain if the count is at home, my lady,' replied the butler who answered the door. He showed them to chairs at the edge of the substantial hallway. A double stairway curved upwards towards a gallery full of family portraits. It was down these stairs that the count's butler floated to inform the ladies that the count would meet them on the veranda.

Lady Gayle and Felicity followed the man as he led them through several sumptuous rooms to the rear of the property. Outside, the veranda gave way to more beautiful formal gardens and a vista over the valley. A haze covered the village below, but the calls of the people working the farmland could be heard as a gentle buzz. The distance making the sounds melodic.

'How may I be of service to two such lovely ladies?'

Lady Gayle turned to face the count. His smile and gracious manners were exquisite, but all the same, as he smoothed his grey moustache, she shivered in the warm sunshine. 'Good morning, Count Bianchi. I wanted to ask about Oliver Thornton,' she said. 'I believe he may work for you. Would you happen to know where he might be?'

The count waved his plump hand towards a table and

chairs under an oversized parasol. 'May I offer you refreshment? My cook makes an excellent lemonade with lemons from my own trees.' He continued his wave to indicate a section of garden given aside to lemon trees. In the centre of the garden, an ancient olive tree, gnarled and twisted, lurked like an old witch in a gathering of fairies.

Puzzled by the slight incongruity of the grouping, Lady Gayle agreed to lemonade. She nodded to Felicity, and they took seats on cushioned chairs underneath the parasol. It was a relief to be out of the bright sunshine.

The count seated himself nearby, and Lady Gayle spent the intervening moments studying him as he poured lemonades into heavy Venetian glasses. She wondered why he had avoided the question about Oliver. Was he buying time before he answered?

He offered small oval-shaped biscuits which looked like madeleines but which were more like thin, crisp lemon shortbread. They were delicious, and for a moment, Lady Gayle almost forgot the reason for their visit.

'Oliver Thornton,' she repeated, raising the intonation at the end of the name to make it sound like a question.

'Oliver came to work for me, yes.' Count Bianchi took a sip from his glass and closed his eyes in pleasure.

'How did he feel when Mr Devine came to stay?'

'I didn't tell him. He did not need to know. I keep my different business interests apart.'

'Were you involved in Imperial Ventures, Count Bianchi? I was given to understand that you *had* decided to invest with them?'

'You have been misled. I was not involved in Imperial Ventures.' Count Bianchi rose, drawing himself to his full height. He pulled his jacket straight, buttoned it and pulled a handkerchief from his pocket. He dabbed at his face.

Lady Gayle glanced at Felicity, who was watching the proceedings, a puzzled look on her face.

'If not Imperial Ventures, then what business did you have with Teddy Devine?' she asked. 'Did you have any business with my uncle too?'

The count didn't answer but ambled to the edge of the veranda and placed his hands on the stone balustrade. 'I was doing it for Oliver,' he said. 'The son of one of my oldest friends. We have a saying in Italy: "Keep your friends close and your enemies closer." I wanted to know what Mr Theodore Devine III had in store next for my young friend.'

The count turned to face them both. 'You see, it wasn't enough that they had ruined Oliver. They blamed him for ruining their business and decided Oliver needed to be punished for the damage he'd caused. Devine chased him here to exact yet more revenge. I could not allow that to happen, but it was easier to ascertain what Devine was up to whilst he was under my roof.' At a rustle of silk behind him, the count glanced in the direction of the noise. He bowed at Julia. 'And I had other incentives.'

Lady Gayle and Felicity glanced in Julia's direction. The former's thoughts instantly returning to the night of the casino visit. Was Julia placing all her bets on this particular horse? But why, if she was as rich as Charles had claimed, why did she need the count? Was she after the title as well? Was that what was important? She watched Julia sway towards the count; his eyes didn't leave her. He was as entranced as any cobra victim, hypnotised by the swaying of her body in time to a music only she could hear.

'Mrs Fitzpatrick, how lovely to see you again,' said Lady

Gayle, and then remembering that Teddy Devine had been her cousin or some other relation. 'How are you feeling?'

'Oh, quite dreadful.' Julia dabbed ineffectually at her eyes with a sliver of lace and linen. 'It's all been a terrible shock. The count has been so kind, helping me make the arrangements to take Teddy back to the States for burial.'

Lady Gayle murmured something she hoped was appropriate but was not taken in by the act. After all, she thought, it's not many people who can sob without tears and puffy eyes.

CHAPTER TWENTY-TWO

As Julia Fitzpatrick prostrated herself in a chair and Count Bianchi fluttered around her, Lady Elizabeth Hansen joined the party on the veranda.

'Makes one feel quite nauseous, doesn't it,' she hissed to Lady Gayle as she poured herself a glass of the lemonade. 'Nonstop arguments when he was alive, and now he's dead, nonstop sobbing.'

Lady Gayle sidled closer. 'I hadn't heard about any arguments,' she whispered. 'What on earth could she and her cousin have had to argue about?'

'I know they weren't cousins, for one thing, and she's not as rich as she likes to make out.'

'How do you know all this?' Over Lady Hansen's shoulder, Lady Gayle signalled to Felicity to ensure she stayed and comforted Julia Fitzpatrick as best she could.

Felicity gave her a quick nod, and Lady Gayle felt able to turn all her attention to the latest witness. She tilted her head to one side and mustered up her best sympathetic face.

'Her undergarments, that's how.'

Lady Gayle lost control of one eyebrow as it shot up towards her hairline. 'Undergarments?'

'I needed a handkerchief. I'd run out, and Julia told me to get one of hers. I wasn't snooping.'

'No, no, of course not,' murmured Lady Gayle.

'Well, when I went into her handkerchief case, I noticed a few frayed items. Something that a good maid would spot and repair without fail. You know the sort of thing?'

Lady Gayle nodded. Alice kept all her clothes immaculate. Although she'd not missed having a maid before, she had no idea how she would manage without Alice's ministrations now. Then she shrugged. She'd manage just fine and simply go back to her old ways. She would cope. She usually had.

Then she realised that Lizzie Hansen was still speaking, and she'd missed something. Giving Lizzie a little smile, she hoped that the gossip would be repeated.

'I think they were both down on their luck. They have nice things and so on, but everything is rather old and worn.'

'You think she's lost her fortune?'

Lady Hansen nodded. 'As far as I can work out, she invested in some scheme of Teddy's, and he lost her money. She's only here now for some other scheme they've cooked up.'

'Such as?'

'An advantageous marriage perhaps?'

'Do you think Count Bianchi knows?'

Lizzie Hansen glanced over to Julia and the count. Lady Gayle followed her gaze. The count continued to fuss around the sobbing woman. 'What do you think?'

In all honesty, Lady Gayle didn't know what to think. Part of her felt sympathetic towards Julia. The woman had, after all, lost a member of her family, and presumably, she had been fond of her cousin, or whatever he was, however much they argued. Another part of her, the more acerbic part, was wondering if it was all an act and, just what had Julia meant when she said she and Earl Harding had been close?

Determined to home in on the truth, Lady Gayle leaned her head towards Lady Hansen. 'What did Mrs Fitzpatrick and Mr Devine argue about?'

'Anything and everything. They were going to sit out of the treasure hunt since they'd devised it and had worked on the clues, but then they had another argument. I helped Julia write the clues on cards in the afternoon. It's also why Julia was with the count, and I was with Teddy in the evening.'

'But you two won. If Teddy knew what all the clues meant, wasn't that cheating.'

Lady Hansen pursed her lips. 'Perhaps,' she said. 'I don't believe he knew all the clues. Julia changed some after he stormed off.'

Lady Gayle frowned for a moment, thinking back to the events of the evening. 'Why did Teddy tear up the clue left on the David statue?'

'I don't know, he said something like, "This will be fun," and he snatched the card from my hand, tore it apart and threw everything in the air.'

'Was that one of the clues you'd written?'

'No, not me. That was one of Julia's. She has quite distinctive handwriting, don't you think?'

Lady Gayle did think. She thought very hard, trying to recollect the handwriting on the cards. Nothing distinctive was coming to mind, but she'd only seen snippets of the card, which was shredded. The only unusual handwriting she'd seen recently was on the half-burnt letters in the fire grate of Bea Harding's bedroom. It gave her a sudden idea.

'Tell me,' she said. 'Did Mrs Fitzpatrick have a close friendship with Earl Harding?'

Lady Hansen mused for a moment, casting her eye over the other group. 'She had been making a play for Richard Harding, or so I'm told. I thought she only knew him through Teddy and Teddy's company. However, since she and Teddy usually argued about money she may have lost her fortune through their company. It would certainly give her a good motive to kill them both, wouldn't it?' Lizzie Hansen snorted with laughter, earning herself a glare from Count Bianchi.

'Would killing them get her fortune back?' said Lady Gayle, although she doubted it. If Charles was correct, the entire Imperial Ventures Group was fraudulent, and Julia Fitzpatrick would only have money again if she married well. Watching her bat her eyelids at the besotted count, clearly, that was her current plan. Whilst Lady Gayle wished her nothing but the best, she had two murders to solve. It was time to divide and conquer.

'Count Bianchi,' she said. 'I wonder if it might be wise for Mrs Fitzpatrick to rest in her room? Felicity and I would be more than happy to ensure she's settled and comfortable. I'm sure Lady Hansen wouldn't mind keeping you company.'

No one looked thrilled by the suggestion, least of all Julia Fitzpatrick, until Lady Gayle whispered in her ear.

After that, the lady was more than happy to retire to her bedroom.

'What do you mean, you think I might be in danger?'

Julia flounced into the room, tossing her handbag on the bed. It bounced off the bed and onto the floor.

'There have been two murders, Mrs Fitzpatrick and you were closely connected to both victims. There's every chance that someone might think you know more than you do.'

'Such as?'

'Why did Earl Harding and Teddy Devine have to die? What do you think might be the reason?' Deciding that Mrs Fitzpatrick wasn't going to pick up the handbag, Lady Gayle did so and placed it on the dressing table. It gave her ample opportunity to notice the frayed and scuffed edges and the clasp, which didn't quite fasten properly.

Lady Hansen was right. Julia Fitzpatrick was down on her luck.

Julia flopped into the chair in front of the dressing table. Opening her handbag, she retrieved a tube of lipstick. She began to apply it whilst using the mirror to stare at Lady Gayle. 'And that's why you think I'm in danger?'

'Well, unless *you* killed them both.'

Julia Fitzpatrick sat back from the mirror. She blotted her lips and twisted in the chair to face Lady Gayle. 'Why would I do that?'

'When we were at the casino, you told me that you and Richard Harding had been close.' Lady Gayle ignored Felicity's sharp intake of breath. 'How close?'

'As close as it's possible for a man and a woman to be.'

'You were lovers?'

Julia nodded.

'But that can't be true,' shouted Felicity. 'I would have known.'

'Would you, my dear?' said Julia. 'Somehow I don't think so.'

'How long has it been going on?' Lady Gayle squeezed Felicity's shoulder, slipping her a handkerchief to wipe away her angry tears.

'Two years? No, nearly three. Then, at Christmas, he told me he couldn't leave his wife. All along, he promised me he'd leave her. Then he decided that he couldn't while she was such a wreck.'

'The cocaine?' whispered Lady Gayle. She glanced at Felicity, wishing there had been a better way for the girl to find out.

'Yes.' Julia nodded. 'He blamed himself.'

'And well he might,' replied Lady Gayle. She crossed to the doorway and let in a maid carrying a tray of lemonade, biscuits and three glasses. 'Were you very angry when he told you that he wasn't leaving Beatrice?'

'At first, yes, I was. Of course, I was. But Teddy said we were coming over here to visit Count Bianchi, and I saw I had another opportunity.' Julia poured herself a glass of the lemonade. She didn't bother offering any to Gayle or Felicity.

'When you came to the villa after Earl Harding was killed, is that why you were so devoid of feelings?'

'Devoid! Is that what you think I was? What a fool you are, Lady Gayle. My heart was breaking, but there was nothing I could do. I had to hide what I was feeling. I had no choice; surely you can see that?' She took a gulp of the lemonade.

'I understand completely,' said Lady Gayle, 'despite how heartless I think you are. Thank you for talking to me.'

She took Felicity by the arm and moved towards the bedroom door, 'By the way,' she said as she opened the door, 'I think you should be careful with anything you eat or drink. You could still be in danger.'

CHAPTER TWENTY-THREE

'Oh, my word. Did you see her face?' Felicity sniggered as they left Julia in her room. 'Do you really think someone's going to poison her?'

'I don't know. All I do know is that you can't be too careful when there's a killer on the loose.'

'What are we doing now?'

'I want to talk to Count Bianchi. On his own if possible. Could you get Lady Hansen to show you around the gardens?'

'You're joking? If you think I'm not going to be in at the kill when you find out who murdered my uncle, you've got another think coming.'

'That's an unfortunate turn of phrase if you don't mind me saying so. Of course, I don't want to leave you out, but I am used to my own way of working.

'I won't get in your way,' announced Felicity, 'but I thought we were a team.'

. . .

However, when they rejoined the count on his veranda, he was alone. Lady Hansen having decided to retire to her room until the day was cooler.

'I wonder, when could we visit your prosciutto factory and vineyard, Count Bianchi?'

'Why, my dear lady,' said the count, rising to his feet. He smiled at them both. 'I would be happy to show you, but perhaps another time. Even though Mrs Fitzpatrick has taken to her room, I cannot, in all good conscience leave her here alone. That is not the behaviour of a good host.'

'Of course not,' replied Lady Gayle. 'I wouldn't dream of asking you to leave poor Julia without company. I think you should remain as her protector; she may still be in danger. Perhaps you could write a little note for us to give to your manager or foreman to ask him to show us around?'

'I still don't understand the need just now.' Reluctantly, Count Bianchi called for his butler to bring paper and a pen. He scribbled a note in a flamboyant hand, the style of which Lady Gayle only glimpsed. He folded the paper over and over again and then dripped red wax onto the rear. He removed his signet ring and pressed it into the hot wax, leaving a distinct impression.

'I do not understand your rush, Lady Gayle,' he said. 'However, these few words give my man Fabio the instructions to show you whatever you need to see. If only you could have waited a few days, we would have made a much more pleasant trip.'

'Two men have been murdered, Count Bianchi. I think the time for pleasant trips out to see the countryside is over.'

Count Bianchi gave her a slight bow as he handed over the missive for the vineyard manager.

Lady Gayle gave him a slight nod as she took instructions. She glanced briefly at his handwriting where he'd written the manager's name, and then beckoning Felicity, the two women left the substantial villa, jumped into the Bugatti, and headed for the hills.

'What are you hoping to find?' Felicity's shouts were barely audible over the Bugatti's engine.

Clasping her cloche hat to her head, Lady Gayle yelled, 'I really don't know. There is, of course, a chance that Oliver has hidden himself away in the vineyard. We do need to question him about his movements on the day that Teddy was killed, but I can't help feeling there's a lot more going on than we've uncovered so far.'

'Such as?' Felicity snatched a look in Lady Gayle's direction, but for the most part, she kept her eyes firmly on the road.

Lady Gayle shook her head. 'Something isn't right. I can't quite put my finger on it. But some things just don't add up.'

Behind the wheel of the powerful car, Felicity shrugged and said nothing more. They climbed higher and higher into the mountains. The air grew colder, and Lady Gayle began to wish she brought a shawl or a jacket.

'Don't you want to check for Oliver at the vineyard?' Felicity didn't take her eyes off the road as she spoke.

'Too obvious,' said Lady Gayle. 'I think Oliver will want to go where no one would think to look for him. Returning to the vineyard would be far too straightforward. It's the first place Commander Ricciardi will go to in search of him. I think we need to rely on places which are far more devious. That's why I asked about the prosciutto farm.'

Lady Gayle relaxed back in the passenger seat as best

she could, considering how far below the valley was and how quickly the Bugatti was speeding around the bends. Just as she thought they were going to run out of road, Felicity swung the powerful car between two large and impressive gateposts. There was, as far as Lady Gayle could see, no fence at all. There were the substantial fence posts and double metal gates which stood open. Over the gateposts hung a sign, Prosciutto Bianchi. It would appear they had arrived.

CHAPTER
TWENTY-FOUR

FELICITY EASED THE CAR DOWN THE DUSTY, POTHOLED TRACK. THE powerful engine spluttered and coughed as if resisting the reduced speed. On either side of the trail, large white pigs wandered around on long, muscular legs. Their floppy ears hung over their eyes, and Lady Gayle wondered how much it obscured their vision.

When they reached the farm buildings, all was quiet. A soft breeze raised by the car tyres caused a small dust storm, whirling strands of hay into a vortex which landed against a barn door. Lady Gayle glanced at her watch and realised they had arrived in the middle of siesta. A break from working in the middle of the day was something she was still getting used to, but even this high up, it was far too hot to work in the baking sun.

She leaned forward and opened the car door, swinging her legs out and pulling herself to a standing position. Once out of the car, she used her handbag to shade her eyes as she looked around for any signs of life.

There was a large, whitewashed building at the edge of the neatly kept yard, which she took to be the farmhouse.

All its windows were covered by heavy wooden shutters to keep out the heat of the day. The front door was ajar, but the interior was dark and still. Lady Gayle peered inside, but there was no answer to her shouts. 'As abandoned as the Marie Celeste,' she called to Felicity. Although, since the door was open, someone must surely be around somewhere.

'What about the barns?' Felicity pointed in the direction of several buildings, and the two women crossed the farm-yard towards them.

The first building contained four sturdy wooden tables with scrubbed tops. On the surface of each one, there was a set of sharp-looking knives. Lady Gayle easily imagined the razor-sharp blades being used to prepare meat. Towards the back of the open space, there were more tables with deep grooves in their centres. As Lady Gayle edged towards these tables, she saw large salt crystals swept into small piles.

'I suppose this is where they apply the salt to the prepared joints,' said Lady Gayle, prodding at the pile of salt.

'Apparently, they massage it into the flesh by hand.'

'How do you know that?' Lady Gayle hoped her voice sounded normal. Coming as it had, so close to her ear, Felicity's voice had made her jump, and she hadn't quite recovered her composure.

'Charles and I had a tour before you arrived. Count Bianchi showed us around. We had the full works. Apparently, they even slaughter the pigs here.'

'What in here?' Lady Gayle sniffed the air and looked around. 'It seems very clean.'

'No, they have another shed they use as the slaughter-house,' said Felicity. 'This region isn't known for its prosciutto, but Count Bianchi thought he'd like to give it a try.'

Lady Gayle nodded. 'Well, Oliver clearly isn't hiding in here.' She glanced over her shoulder at the tables of knives. After the heat of the sun, it was very cool inside the brick-built barn, and she shivered. 'If you've had a look round before, where do you think he might be hiding?'

'Haybarn?' Felicity turned on her heel to leave the processing barn, and Lady Gayle followed.

Glancing at the knives as she walked past; she idly counted them. There's one missing, she murmured to herself, spotting the gap. There must be a good explanation, she decided as she dismissed the thought, but all the same, a shiver ran down her spine.

Once outside in the warm sunshine, she rubbed her arms vigorously to chase away the chills. Two buildings down from the processing barn was an oak-built structure with tall wooden doors that were pushed closed. Felicity headed straight to this building as if she knew exactly where she was going; she pulled one door open wide enough for them to slip through. Two rats squealed and fled from the barn.

Lady Gayle glowered after them with a shudder. 'I hate rats,' she muttered.

'Yes, me too,' said Felicity as she ducked through the gap in the door.

The smell of the haybarn was intoxicating. Lady Gayle stared up at the bales of hay piled one on top of the other. From windows high up near the roof of the barn, sunlight flooded in, and dust motes hanging in the air were illuminated by the shafts of light. Like the rest of the farm, this space gave no indication of human habitation. It was utterly deserted.

Felicity turned to Lady Gayle with a shrug. 'This is the most comfortable place. Certainly, it's where I'd hide away, but let's search the other two as well.'

'Very well.' Lady Gayle followed Felicity to a third barn. It was as clean as the preparation shed, stacked high with salt sacks and materials for packing the prepared hams. It was empty too.

Felicity nodded towards the final shed. 'I didn't like this one,' she said. When they sneaked in, it was clear what had caused Felicity's unease.

The sharp tang of bleach didn't quite mask the stench of blood, death, and fear. There was no indication that anyone was hiding there.

'I still think the haybarn is our best bet. I'll climb up into the loft and check.'

They returned to the barn with its delicious scent of dried mown grass. Felicity clambered up the rickety ladder into the loft, but after a few minutes, she returned shaking her head.

'Botheration,' hissed Lady Gayle. 'Where can he have got to? I was convinced he'd secreted himself away somewhere like this.'

'I was hoping the same. I was certainly hoping you'd lead me to him.'

Felicity and Lady Gayle whirled around. In front of them, his gun trained on them both, was the Pinkerton detective.

'Why Mr Cornwall. Oh, my apologies, Mr Martins. Are you following us?' Lady Gayle backed away, trying to push Felicity behind her. 'Why on earth would you feel the need to do that?'

'A Pinkerton always gets his man,' said the detective. He smoothed back his hair and glanced around as if his quarry were hiding in the shadows. 'Theodore Devine had embezzled money from his employers, and it's my job to get that money back.'

'It was my understanding that the Imperial Ventures group belonged to Mr Devine, Mr Cornwall.' Lady Gayle put her hands on her hips. 'What *is* your real name? Cornwall? Or Martins?'

The Pinkerton smiled ruefully, 'Daniel Martins, at your service, ma'am. Although my dear old mom always called me Danny.'

'That still doesn't really explain why you're here and why you're in pursuit of Oliver.'

'That's something I'd like to know too.'

Lady Gayle stiffened. Gosh, he did that quietly, she thought. Her gaze had been entirely on the detective, and she'd missed Oliver, hiding in the shadows and creeping in through the half-open door. As he stepped closer, a shaft of sunlight glinted on something metallic.

The missing knife.

CHAPTER TWENTY-FIVE

'Oliver, it doesn't have to be like this.' Lady Gayle spoke softly. 'Put the knife down.'

Oliver didn't glance in her direction. He simply changed his grip on the weapon. With his fingertips on the point of the blade, he was poised to throw. His narrowed eyes were fixed on the detective who, with his back to danger, still clasped his pistol.

Lady Gayle shrugged at the detective. Danny Martins returned the gesture and leaned forward, allowing the pistol to drop to the floor. Then he turned around to face Oliver, his hands slightly raised. 'Come on, buddy, we just want to know why you killed Teddy.'

Lady Gayle sighed. She was confident that Oliver had nothing to do with Teddy's death. He was a hothead, that much was certain, but only a skilled driver could have driven Teddy's car off that narrow road without injuring themselves. There was only one such driver that she knew of, and it was a jolly good job that Felicity had been with her at the time, otherwise, *she* would be the prime suspect. 'Oliver, you mustn't worry,' she said, 'Felicity and I know you're not responsible for Mr Devine's death, but we do want to hear your side of the story.'

Beside her, she heard Felicity mutter, 'We do?'

Lady Gayle nodded and motioned Felicity to be quiet.

Oliver glanced in Lady Gayle's direction. 'I didn't do it. I didn't kill either of them, but no one will believe me. I don't want to hang.' His shoulders slumped.

'I won't let that happen, but you must tell me where you were when Teddy crashed. But if you can't remember that, perhaps you could tell me where you were when Earl Harding was killed?'

Oliver shrugged. 'I'm so tired,' he said. His entire body sagged, and he let the knife slip from his hand. The clatter echoed in the silent barn. Instantly, Martins jumped upon Oliver and forced him to the ground. 'I should arrest you for wasting my time,' Martins growled. 'Now, be a good boy and tell the lady where you were.'

Face pressed into the hard-packed earth of the barn floor; Oliver was unable to speak, but he shook his head.

'Let him up, Mr Martins,' said Lady Gayle. 'He can't speak with a mouthful of dust.'

The Pinkerton eased his grip, and Oliver twisted onto his right side and faced his inquisitors. 'Tell Lady Gayle where you were,' Martins repeated.

Oliver shook his head again. 'I don't know,' he said. 'My memory isn't as good as it used to be. I wake up in strange places and can't remember how I got there.'

'I see.' Lady Gayle chewed at her lip. Memory gaps were not uncommon with people who were heavy drinkers, that much she did know. She'd experienced it herself when blocking out her grief over her husband's death. 'What *can* you remember? Where did you wake up?'

Oliver shrugged and rubbed his hands over his eyes. 'I

don't know. There are times when I don't even know what day it is.'

Lady Gayle looked at the Pinkerton still sitting on Oliver's legs. 'He's not our man.'

'How can you be so sure?'

'Because I believe him about the memory gaps. Count Bianchi told me he'd given Oliver his last chance. I think this is the reason Oliver began to drink heavily on Tuesday.'

'You think he's got an alibi because he was on a bender?' hissed Felicity. 'Are you sure?'

'I'm quite sure,' replied Lady Gayle. 'Remember how drunk he was when we saw him at the casino?'

'He was pretty sozzled,' agreed Felicity.

'He was indeed.' Lady Gayle regarded Oliver with a baleful eye. 'I think Oliver was too drunk to drive safely. Driving Teddy off the road was no accident, was it? How many people, apart from you, could do that and not crash their own car?'

'Not many.'

'You can let him go,' Lady Gayle said to the Pinkerton.

Martins glowered at her, but all the same, he rose to his feet and brushed off some of the barn floor dust from his trousers. He didn't help Oliver to scrabble to his feet. 'What now?' he said.

'Felicity and I will escort Oliver back to the village and leave him with Miss Blues. If I see Commander Ricciardi, I will tell him we've found Oliver, but only if I see him.'

'You can't do that,' Oliver burst out. 'He'll arrest me. He won't listen to reason. His sort never do.'

Lady Gayle carried on speaking as if she hadn't heard him. 'I'd like to find out where *you* were at the time of both murders, Mr Martins.'

'Me? You can't possibly suspect me?'

'I think at this stage, Mr Martins, pretty much anyone is a suspect, don't you?' She folded her arms and glared at the Pinkerton. 'Felicity, please could you help Oliver to the car?'

Felicity trudged to where Oliver was still on the floor. She pulled him to his feet and began to propel him outside. 'Don't start questioning the Pinkerton until I'm back,' she muttered.

Lady Gayle had been on the point of doing just that, but she relented. 'Of course not, Felicity,' she murmured. 'I wouldn't dream of it.' She followed Felicity into the farmyard.

A tanned and muscled man was strolling from the farmhouse. He was pulling a shirt over his head. He tucked it into his trousers and pulled his elasticated braces onto his shoulders. He stopped and scratched his head when he saw the party of people exiting his barn.

'I think it might be a good idea if Oliver is kept out of this,' said Lady Gayle. 'That must be Fabio. I should give him Count Bianchi's note.' She strode over to the man and gave him the message that Count Bianchi had sent for him.

He read it but still looked confused. 'We won't be needing the tour now,' said Lady Gayle in her best Italian.

The man nodded slowly. He folded his arms and stared down at Lady Gayle; she returned the stare. Then, the man shook his head and wandered to the pump in the centre of the yard. He placed the note in a pocket, sluiced water over his head, and, after rubbing his head and face, he stood upright and shook the water out of his hair.

Felicity watched the entire show, a slow smile forming on her face. 'I wonder if we should all return to the village and talk there,' she said. 'There might be fewer distractions.'

Glancing at the count's man, Lady Gayle said. 'Yes, you

could be right. Let's go back. Are you still happy to drive with Oliver while I travel with Mr whatever he's called?'

'What? You can't be serious. I thought we were a team?' Felicity glowered. Her eyes narrowed, and she flushed.

'Getting Oliver to safety is an important job. I don't trust that Pinkerton enough to leave him on his own. I need you to do this, Felicity. You're the only one I trust right now.'

'It still feels like you're cutting me out. I'll do what you ask, but I'm not happy about it.' She pushed Oliver into the Bugatti, jumped in and drove away, leaving everyone in a cloud of her dust.

CHAPTER
TWENTY-SIX

While Mr Martins followed the Bugatti down to Montecielo, Lady Gayle allowed several ideas to flow through her mind. Wishing that Alice was there to talk things over with, she began to count the suspects off on her fingers.

There were a number of contenders for the role of Earl Harding's murderer. Felicity she had discounted on account of she herself was Felicity's alibi for both murders.

Bea Harding she had already discounted as Charles was *her* alibi for the Earl's murder and, since she wasn't a motor car driver, she could not have committed the second.

Charles? Lady Gayle put her head back on the seat rest. No, she would discount Charles, if only because she'd suspected him in the past and had had to apologise. No, she would not be doing that again. In any case, Charles was with Countess Harding when the Earl was killed. So that ruled him out.

She went through the rest of her list. Jane Blues. Julia Fitzpatrick. Count Bianchi. Everyone had an alibi for one of the two murders. Although she was convinced that both deaths were the actions of one person, Lady Gayle realised that she had to face the possibility that there were two killers in their midst. She shivered despite the warmth of the day. It was not a thought she relished. Not at all.

It was with some surprise Lady Gayle realised they had arrived in Montecielo. Mr Martins drew his small black car to a halt in the centre of the square.

She caught sight of Charles chatting with Jane Blues in the café, and she smiled to herself. Charles always managed to find the prettiest woman around and convince her to spend time with him. Lady Gayle didn't wait for Mr Martins to open her door for her, which was probably just as well since he headed straight into the café without giving her a backward glance.

'Well, really,' she sighed, whilst thinking that perhaps it was merely a sign of modern times. Or perhaps Mr Martins wanted to spend time with Miss Blues too and was jealous of Charles getting all the attention.

She alighted from the small car, shaking out her dress to remove the creases and dust from the journey. Eyes shaded, Lady Gayle glanced up at the clear sky. The sun was relentless even though it was past siesta, and the day should be getting cooler. She toyed with the idea of buying a pair of the shaded glasses Julia Fitzpatrick and Bea Harding favoured. *I wonder where they buy them?*

She sighed as she watched the detective head straight for the table where Charles and Jane were seated. Yet, to her surprise, it didn't appear that he wanted to speak to Jane at all. He sat himself at the table, ignoring the young woman and addressed his questions to Charles.

'What on earth is he up to?' she muttered to herself as

she approached the table. Ordering chilled water with ice and lemon for herself, Lady Gayle took a seat next to Jane Blues.

'I expect you're wondering what gives?' Jane leaned over to her and whispered in her ear.

'I am rather.' Lady Gayle thanked the waiter and took a sip of the water he had poured for her. She wiped her chilled fingers with a paper napkin and rested the glass back on the table. 'What does give?' she asked, hoping that her words were the correct response to Jane's comment.

Jane giggled. 'What gives?' she said. 'That's what you're supposed to say. And what gives, is that this here Pinkerton is accusing Lord Charles of being party to Earl Harding's and Teddy's Ponzi scheme. Naturally, Lord Charles is denying it all.'

'Naturally,' murmured Lady Gayle. She wracked her brain to recall what on earth a Ponzi scheme was, and then the name came to her. Charles Ponzi was the man who'd deliberately swindled people out of their money with some scheme or other. She recalled the news from two or three years earlier. Ponzi used the cash from new investors to provide dividends to earlier investors. It was exactly what Richard and Teddy had been doing. She wondered if they'd stolen the idea from Ponzi himself. With what she knew about them now, she wouldn't put it past either of them. 'Charles mentioned that Earl Harding's and Teddy's company wasn't making a profit.'

'Yes, he said as much to this detective before you arrived. It's just that this Pinkerton...' Jane said the name with intense distaste, 'thinks that Charles had a hand in it all.'

'Surely not—' Lady Gayle began, but then she stopped. Was she sure? She looked at Charles. As usual, his poker face gave nothing away, but there was a sheen that, even in this heat, she'd not noticed before. But no, Charles had promised her he'd had nothing to do with Imperial Ventures.

As if noticing her staring, Charles glanced in Lady Gayle's direction. He gave her the flicker of a smile, which he extended to Jane as well.

For a reason she could not fully understand, Lady Gayle didn't find herself in the least bit reassured. She sat back and watched the battle before her.

Danny Martins placed his elbows on the table and leaned towards Charles Vickery. 'Viscount Vickery, I know what was going on at Imperial Ventures. I know about the Ponzi fraud. Like Lady Gayle here, I suspect that's what got both Earl Harding and Teddy Devine killed. Are you next?'

Charles blanched; his face became ashen under his tan. 'I don't believe so. I removed myself and my money from Imperial Ventures in early '21. Just as soon as I realised what they were up to.'

'But you stayed friendly with them. Why? Why are you staying here in Tuscany with them? Don't you have other friends in the area that you can stay with?'

Lady Gayle's eyes flicked towards Charles. She knew the reason he remained friendly with Bea Harding, but he would never reveal the truth.

Lord Charles sighed. He was regaining his composure. 'I felt sorry for Bea Harding,' he said. 'Richard could be quite... let's just say, he could be quite harsh with her. She needed support at times.'

'Is that support in the form of white powder, Lord Charles?'

'No, of course not,' replied Charles. 'I'm not some common drug dealer.'

Lady Gayle dipped her head, knowing that if Mr Martins glimpsed her face, it would reveal the truth. Whilst she could maintain a reasonable visage while playing poker, she was unable to lie convincingly.

'I think that's exactly what you are, Lord Charles. You supply cocaine, and heaven alone knows what else to the rich and famous. That's why you receive invitations to stay in places like the Villa Montagna Verde. That's why you maintain such powerful friends. Well, I'm here to tell you, Lord Charles—'

'Thank you, Mr Martins.' Lady Gayle rose from her seat and placed her hand on the Pinkerton's arm. 'I don't think you should make baseless accusations to Viscount Vickery. Charles, if there is anything you can tell me about either death, it would be helpful. I don't believe you're involved, but nor do I think that Oliver had a hand in either death. We must get to the bottom of this and make sure justice is served.'

'I quite agree, Gigi,' replied Charles. 'However, I don't think I can help you. I was nowhere near Teddy's car accident, and as for Richard's death... there's nothing I can tell you. I went to find some champagne, and I thought Bea remained in the sitting room.'

'It must have been quite some explosion when you opened the champagne if it soaked her dress so badly she needed to change.' Lady Gayle studied Charles' face for a response, but as usual, he gave nothing away. He simply gave the briefest of shrugs without any reply before he walked away.

CHAPTER TWENTY-SEVEN

'Oh, there you both are.' Lady Gayle lifted her head to look in the direction of the speaker.

Felicity pushed Oliver into a chair with his back to the rest of the café. 'I went to your apartment, Janie, but you weren't there. Your brute of a brother wouldn't let Oliver in. We've been driving around for ages. I hadn't got a clue what to do with him. I was terrified that I would run into the police.'

Oliver slouched in the chair with his head in his hands. 'I can't be seen here. Can we go?'

Jane rose. 'Of course,' she said. 'We'll go to the club.' She signalled a waiter, whispered to him quietly, then she and Oliver left the café via the kitchen.

Silence fell over the table as Felicity, Lady Gayle and Danny Martins stared at each other. 'What are your plans now, Mr Martins? I don't think you have any further questions for Viscount Vickery, do you?'

The Pinkerton opened his mouth but shut it again. He shook his head.

'Good, but now that Teddy is dead, your job must be

over. It's not as though *you* can bring him to justice now. Will you return to America?'

The Pinkerton rubbed his hands over his face and through his hair. 'That may not be a good idea.'

Lady Gayle and Felicity exchanged glances.

'You can't leave us in suspense like that,' said Felicity. 'Are you under a death threat?'

Martins coughed. He ordered a whisky and ice from the waiter. He snatched the glass from the tray and had sunk half the spirit before the waiter had registered he was holding an empty tray. 'Yes,' he said and drank the remainder of the whisky.

'You don't think you can leave it there, do you? You have to tell us the rest of the story,' said Felicity.

Martins glanced at Lady Gayle, and she raised her eyebrows at him. 'It might be for the best.'

'Even if it shows your pal Lord Charles in a bad light?' Martins twisted his glass around in the condensation puddle on the table.

'Oh rather,' said Felicity with enthusiasm. 'We've always suspected Charles was up to no good when he was in the Americas.'

'He wasn't.' Martins snapped his fingers, and the waiter brought another whisky over. 'Do you ladies want anything?'

Both women shook their heads. 'Probably best if you get it off your chest,' prompted Lady Gayle.

Martins nodded. 'We Pinkertons get engaged to do all sorts of unusual jobs. The sort of things that are outside the purview of the police and to some extent—'

'The law?' interjected Felicity.

Martins tilted his head to one side as he looked at her. Then he pursed his lips and carried on as if the interruption hadn't happened. 'I was asked to investigate Theodore Devine III by an insurance company. His father hadn't heard from his son for some months. There were concerns that Teddy may have met an untimely end. This particular insurance company was especially keen to find Teddy. We often take on missing persons cases, and at first, this one was no different from any others that I'd handled.'

Felicity opened her mouth to ask the obvious question, but Lady Gayle shushed her with a quick glance.

'Yes,' Martins said. 'You clocked it. At first. After a while, it was clear that there was much more going on. My boss at the agency tried to contact Teddy's father, but Mr Devine II was never available. That's not *all* that odd. He's a busy man, but the longer it went on, the more suspicious my boss became. In the end, I visited the old man at his bank in New York.

'He'd never asked for us to investigate Teddy's disappearance at all. The insurance company was all a ruse. Mr Devine didn't even know Teddy was missing.'

'Are father and son estranged?' asked Lady Gayle.

'No, they just don't get on too good and as long as Teddy was still spending his allowance, his father just assumed he was fine.'

'But he wasn't?'

'No, he was not. He was in hiding. The people really looking for Teddy were the Bruno-Scarfo family. They're an organised crime syndicate. Mafia. You heard of the mafia?'

'I've read about organised crime,' said Lady Gayle. She looked at Felicity, who nodded.

'You wouldn't believe who gets involved in car racing.'

'What did this family, is that what they call themselves, a family? What did they want with Teddy?'

'He was laundering money for them. Or at least that's

what he was supposed to be doing. But he wasn't very good at it. All he had to do was take their money, buy businesses like restaurants, hotels, and apartment blocks, and fake the income so that the family looked like they were making lots of money legally.'

'What went wrong?'

Martins shrugged and looked around for the waiter. He signalled for another whisky. 'Teddy got greedy. He thought he could make even more money. So, instead of buying the places he was told to, he started buying others that the family hadn't approved. That's when he started losing money. He tried to bring in investors, but he lost their money too.

'In some ways, I felt sorry for him, but he just got himself in deeper and deeper. He tried to get Charles involved, and then he met Richard Harding.'

'Earl Harding then got the aristocracy involved and lost their money. We know all this, and I still don't see how it stops you from returning home.'

Martins snatched the whisky from the waiter's tray and gulped it down. He wiped his mouth with the back of his hand. 'They wanted Teddy dead and made it quite clear that I was the one they wanted to do the job.'

'You agreed to kill Teddy?' Lady Gayle stared at the detective. Her steely blue eyes widening with shock. 'How... why would you agree to do that?'

Martins shrugged, staring into the glass. 'I had no choice.'

'There's always a choice, Mr Martins. However, now that Teddy is dead, surely this crime family have got what they wanted?'

'You'd think so, but it doesn't cancel out my debts to them.'

'You owe them money? Are you a gambler, Mr Martins?'

The Pinkerton shook his head. His face creased as if he was in pain. 'No, not me. My little sister. They've got their hooks into her. I had to promise to kill Teddy to save her.'

'I see.' Lady Gayle leaned away from the table. While her face remained expressionless, there was a flicker of empathy in her eyes. She'd never had a sister, and her brother had been killed in 1915, but she could still understand the need to save one's family. Regardless of what they had done. 'Then surely you have a responsibility to go back and face the music to save your sister?'

'It's too late.' Martins twisted the empty glass in his hands. His voice cracked. 'I got a wire this morning. She's already dead.'

Lady Gayle opened her mouth to offer sympathy. Then she recalled how she'd felt on hearing about Alfred's death at Ypres. She reached across and squeezed Martins' hand.

CHAPTER TWENTY-EIGHT

Lady Gayle rose from the table and placed some lire notes under the vase of flowers. She patted Danny Martins on the shoulder. 'We're going back to the villa now. Try not to drink too much. Perhaps you could join us for dinner later if you feel up to it.'

Felicity rose too. She glanced at Lady Gayle with a "what do we do now?" expression clouding her face, but there was no answer forthcoming as her ladyship headed towards the door.

Once outside, Felicity's face creased into a frown. 'Is it safe to leave him like that?'

'It's less than ideal, Felicity, but we can't forget we still have a murder to solve. His suggestion that Charles could be next has made me very worried—'

'But Charles can take care of himself.'

'I know he can, but if anything were to happen to him, would that thought comfort you?'

Felicity shook her head.

'I thought not. Now let's go back to the villa, and we can go through all our clues again.'

'We weren't very smart on the treasure hunt clues. What makes you think we'll be any better at this?'

Lady Gayle giggled. 'Firstly, experience and secondly, we gave up on the treasure hunt because someone cheated; not because we weren't any good. There's also the fact that I like to talk things over with Alice. She always has a different perspective on life.'

The two women jumped into the Bugatti and drove back to the villa. When they arrived, Alice reported that Countess Harding was having a lie down, and there had been no sign of Lord Charles.

'How has she been, Alice? Has she slept or eaten?'

'She's not been too well, milady. Not a morsel has passed her lips. She keeps asking about Lord Charles though.'

'Has she run out of her snow?'

Alice nodded. 'I believe she's just taken the last of it. Is that why she keeps asking for Lord Charles?'

Lady Gayle nodded. 'Have there been any callers?'

Alice produced a letter that had been placed on the mantelshelf in the sitting room. 'This came a couple of hours ago. And I found something else I thought you'd find interesting.'

Lady Gayle took the letter and the bulky sachet from her maid. She scanned the handwriting before glancing at Alice, who nodded. Then she passed the slim envelope to Felicity and dropped the sachet on a table. 'Have you seen this writing before?'

'I think so,' said Felicity with a frown. 'That last clue from the treasure hunt. Wasn't that written like this?'

'I believe you're right. But there's something else. Alice, could you bring that snippet of paper we rescued from the fire?

Alice bobbed and dashed out the room. She was back in moments with the half-burned scrap of paper. In the meantime, Lady Gayle had taken the envelope from Felicity. She opened it and read the letter. As she'd expected, it was from Julia Fitzpatrick, and when she checked the handwriting against that in the burned document, both samples matched exactly.

'But we already know Julia was the one writing to Uncle Richard. She told us that before we went to find Oliver. I'd like to know who burned the letters, though and why?'

'You forget where we found the letters, Felicity,' said Lady Gayle with a tight smile. 'I think from what Mrs Fitzpatrick told us earlier today, she hadn't given up on Earl Harding and was trying to rekindle the affair.'

Charles leaned against the sitting room door. 'I told you a while ago that they were letters from a lady to her lover.'

Lady Gayle jumped. 'Where did you spring from, Charles? We were looking for you earlier.'

'I'm here now,' he said. 'What are you up to?'

Lady Gayle passed him the letter, and he ran his eyes over the words, handing it back with a slight raising of his eyebrows.

'Is that why Julia wants to see us now? Does she want to confess?' Felicity placed her hands on her hips.

'I rather suspect she's had time to think things over, and she's worked out who did kill Earl Harding. No doubt she wants to tell us all about it.'

'We should send someone to fetch Commander Ricciardi,' said Lord Charles. 'I'll send Giuseppe.' He turned to leave the room, but, to the surprise of the women, instead of departing, he backed slowly into the room.

Bea Harding held a revolver to Charles' head in shaking hands. 'No one is going anywhere,' she said.

'Bea, don't be so foolish. Put the gun down. We can talk about this.'

'What is there to talk about, Lady Gayle,' sneered the countess. She supported her gun hand with her left hand. 'Surely you've worked it out by now?'

'Yes, you're quite right, Countess Harding. I have worked it out. There were still some things I wanted to slot into place, but I suppose now is as good a time as any.' Lady Gayle smiled at the countess and then at the rest of the room. From the corner of her eye, she saw Alice sneak behind the curtain covering the French windows. She sighed with relief when the curtains stopped fluttering in the breeze. Alice had escaped and would alert the commander.

'As soon as I arrived I felt something strange was afoot. Earl Harding was always so attentive to you, wasn't he, Countess?'

'What of it? Richard and I were deeply in love even after ten years of marriage.'

Lady Gayle shook her head and held out the note from Julia Fitzpatrick. 'Earl Harding had a mistress. You'd found the letters, but they were unsigned. You didn't know who the sender was, at least not until the night of the treasure hunt.

'That's when you saw the same handwriting on the clues. You knew Julia and Lizzie Hansen had written the clues. But Richard's mistress had been here in Montecielo before Lizzie arrived, so you knew it wasn't Lizzie. It's why you arranged to come back from the treasure hunt early—to confront Richard.'

'Nonsense. You're talking absolute rot.' The countess hefted the gun again. Unused to its weight, it was getting the better of her. 'In any case, Charles was with me the entire time from our return from the treasure hunt to you arriving, and we all found my poor husband's body together.'

'No, that's not quite true.' Charles lowered his hands and shook the blood back into them. 'You were alone for nearly half an hour while I went to fetch some champagne. I needed to find the key to the cellar, a light, champagne glasses. I was gone ages. When I got back, you'd changed your dress.'

'I changed, Charles, because you spilt champagne on me. The bottles weren't properly chilled, and the first one bubbled over when it was opened.'

Charles frowned. 'Yes, that's true,' he began, 'but you didn't change your dress. You'd already changed. I remember now. I didn't mention it at the time. Well, well, one doesn't, does one? Seems a bit impertinent to remark on a lady changing her clothes, especially if that lady isn't one's wife.'

'Oh, do be quiet, Charles. No one wants to listen to your ramblings, and for goodness' sake, put your hands up again.' The countess narrowed her eyes.

Charles raised his hands once more. He dropped them as soon as Lady Gayle signalled him to do so.

'She's not going to shoot you, Charles. The gun isn't loaded.'

Open-mouthed, Countess Harding wrenched the barrel of the revolver open. Her face blanched when she saw the empty chambers. Furious and confused, she turned to Lady Gayle, who poured the contents of the sachet Alice had passed her earlier into her cupped hand.

'Are you missing something?' Lady Gayle jiggled the bullets in her left hand.

'You think you're so clever, don't you?'

Lady Gayle shook her head, 'Not me. My maid Alice. She saw the gun, and she retrieved the bullets to give to me. The fact you had a loaded gun confirmed all my suspicions about you.'

Countess Beatrice looked around the room. Her head darting from side to side. 'Where is Alice? She was here a moment ago. She's always sneaking around. I wonder how you can stand it.'

Thinking of Fredericks, her unobtrusive butler at Bethencourt Castle, Lady Gayle smiled. It had taken her some time to become used to how he popped up just when she needed him. 'Alice will be back soon. I asked her to find something for me.'

'And she has found it, your ladyship.'

The countess whirled around. Behind her, their pistols aimed at her with unshaking hands, stood the black-shirted police officer and the Pinkerton detective. Commander Alessandro Ricciardi and Danny Martins were side by side.

CHAPTER TWENTY-NINE

'I think you should perhaps take a seat, Countess Harding,' said Commander Ricciardi. 'I shall take a seat next to you.'

'What are *they* all doing here?' Ignoring the commander's comments, Beatrice Harding sneered as Julia Fitzpatrick, Count Bianchi, Jane Blues, and Oliver Thornton strolled into the tiny sitting room. It was quite a squeeze, especially on a warm night.

'I couldn't say,' replied Lady Gayle. 'I only sent for the commander.' She raised an eyebrow at him.

'I read it in a book,' he said. 'It seemed like a good idea to bring all the suspects together. Shall I begin?'

Lady Gayle shook her head. 'I think I'd prefer to go first. If you don't mind, Commander?'

'Very well.' He bowed, clicking the heels of his boots together. 'As you wish. Ladies first.'

Lady Gayle faced her audience. Her mouth was dry, and she coughed. Charles passed her a glass of water; she took a sip but kept the glass in her hand.

'When I arrived a short while ago, I was presented with

an image of the perfect marriage. The Hardings were a blissfully happy couple, totally enamoured and wrapped up in each other. Or at least that's what I was shown, but it didn't take long for the veil to fall, and the cracks began to show.

'At first glance, it appeared Earl Richard Harding was the perfect husband. He always had a kind word for his wife, a quick smile, but after a few days, I noticed that he rarely spent more than a few minutes a day in her company.'

'He was working. He worked extremely hard,' snarled Beatrice Harding.

'Yes, he was. Richard Harding worked tirelessly. He rarely appeared for meals, and he said he had no time for evening entertainments. However, that wasn't due to his work, but because he had a mistress.'

'Liar!'

Lady Gayle ignored the interruption, although she gave Bea Harding a sympathetic smile. 'I returned to my room one evening when I smelt burning. Burning paper has quite a distinctive smell, and I was quite sure no one would be lighting a fire in their rooms. Not in this heat. I realised there was a good chance that someone was destroying something, but it was none of my business, and I simply filed it away in my mind.' She glanced at the countess, who sat twisting her hands in her lap.

Taking another sip of water, Lady Gayle carried on. 'Then we come to the night of the treasure hunt. Once again, Earl Harding didn't join the party. He was far too busy with work, or at least that's what he told us.'

'He *was* busy,' announced Bea Harding. 'You all heard him say that.'

'Yes, Countess, we all heard what he said, but it was a

lie.' Lady Gayle pointed her glass at Countess Harding. 'You, above all people, knew it was a lie.

'We went to the restaurant, and all ate dinner together. Then, after dinner, we paired up to begin the treasure hunt. Countess Harding, as I recall, you were with Lord Charles because you said you don't drive?'

'That's correct. I am not a motorcar driver.'

Lady Gayle nodded. 'We'll come back to that,' she said. She took another sip of water, cradling the glass in her hands. 'One of the clues seemed to upset you, didn't it, Countess Harding? Why was that?'

'Nothing upset me,' declared the countess. 'Just ask Charles.'

Turning to face Viscount Vickery, Lady Gayle raised a single eyebrow. 'Do you want to tell your side of the story, Charles?'

Charles sighed before pinching the bridge of his nose. 'Gigi, is this entirely necessary?'

'It is,' said Lady Gayle.

'Very well. After the debacle in the park, when Teddy tore up the final clue, Bea was rather upset. I didn't know what the trouble was. We were able to piece the card back together and read the clue, but she wanted to come back early, and so that's what we did.'

'Would you care to share what upset you? After all, you said you weren't upset, but Lord Charles has just said you were. Which was it, Countess Harding?'

The Countess hung her head, her eyes fixed on her clasped hands. 'Very well. I was upset. We came back early.'

'What upset you?'

'It was the handwriting. I'd seen it before.'

'On the letters that you burnt in your room?'

Countess Harding nodded as a single tear dripped from her face onto her hands.

'What did you do when you returned to the villa? Did you confront your husband?'

'Of course not! I wanted to gather my thoughts first.'

'Gather your thoughts? Or did you want to take a sniff of the white powder you favour? Or perhaps both? Tell me, Countess, how did you persuade Earl Harding to come down to the fountain?' Lady Gayle placed her glass down and hugged herself, clasping her elbows in the opposite hands.

Countess Harding raised her head, blinking tears away. 'My doctor prescribed Veronal for me, to help me sleep. I popped some in Richard's brandy before we went out. I suspected he'd planned to meet his mistress, and I wanted him to miss their appointment by sleeping past the time they'd arranged to meet.'

'However, when you returned to the villa,' said Lady Gayle, 'you had worked out who his mistress was, hadn't you?'

'I had,' replied the countess. 'I was furious with him. When I found the letters, I realised the affair had been going on for some time. Then I saw her handwriting on the treasure hunt clues. That's when I realised she was here; I also knew exactly who she was.' Countess Harding rose and dashed towards Julia Fitzpatrick, her hands held out; her curled fingers with their sharp nails looked like claws.

Commander Ricciardi acted quickly, and he grabbed the Countess around the waist before she could attack the other woman. He pushed her into a chair and stood over her.

'I acted on impulse,' panted Countess Bea. 'You just saw what I'm like. I didn't plan any of this.'

'That's not quite true though, is it?' said Lady Gayle. 'You've been planning for days. That's why you arranged for the fountain to be full of water, so you could persuade Richard out into the courtyard so you could drown him.'

'Repairing the fountain was your idea, Lady Gayle. It was nothing to do with me.' Countess Harding gave her a serene smile.

'It was though. It *was* your idea,' Felicity burst out. 'You've been going on about the fountain even before Lady Gayle got here. You just made us think it was our idea.'

'She's been very clever, Felicity,' said Lady Gayle. 'Very clever indeed. But once she'd killed once, it was easy to kill again. Why did Teddy have to die? Was it because he introduced Richard and Julia?'

'She can't drive though,' said Charles. 'We know from the old man with the donkey cart that Teddy's car was forced off the road by another car.'

'More evidence of how clever the Countess has been. She has allowed us to believe that she can't drive, but that's not true. Don't you remember her saying about driving a general in his staff car during the war? It's not that Countess Beatrice Harding *can't* drive; it's simply that she *doesn't* drive any longer.'

'You b—. I'll scratch your eyes out.' Restrained as she was by Commander Ricciardi, Countess Harding was unable to reach Lady Gayle to scratch her. A fact for which Lady Gayle was truly grateful.

CHAPTER THIRTY

'Come along, Countess Harding,' said Commander Ricciardi, reaching down to clasp her elbow. 'I think everyone will feel much more comfortable if you accept my hospitality.'

'You're arresting me?' Open-mouthed, Countess Harding struggled to release herself from his grasp. 'You have no evidence. What Gayle has said is pure conjecture. Ask her to prove it.'

The commander released a long sigh. He looked at Lady Gayle, 'Do you have any solid evidence?'

'We have her dress,' said Lady Gayle.

'But surely that has dried by now?'

Lady Gayle glanced at Alice, who gave her a quick nod. She left the room, returning almost instantly with the gown Countess Harding had worn on the evening of the treasure hunt. She passed it to her mistress.

'Yes, commander, you're quite correct, the dress has dried. However, what you can see here are the stains left by the water in the fountain.' Lady Gayle held the dress up for everyone to see. A wavy pale green line showed against the white silk. 'Cleaning silk has to be done very carefully. There's always a danger of leaving a watermark. What you can see here, Commander, is a watermark, and the staining is caused by the copper sulphate used to treat the water in the fountain. There's nowhere else in the villa or nearby where there's a body of water treated with copper sulphate. The fountain is the only place she could have soaked her dress and ruined it in this manner.'

'And the car? Where did she get a car from?'

Lady Gayle turned to Count Bianchi. 'The car you loaned Lord Charles on the night of the treasure hunt, where is it?'

Count Bianchi shrugged. 'I have no idea,' he said. 'I told Lord Charles he could keep the car for as long as he was staying here.'

Lord Charles shook his head. 'I didn't check on the car. Why would I? It never occurred to me that someone would take it.'

'Didn't you see it being driven away from the villa?' said Lady Gayle.

'I can't say as I did. I didn't expect it to be pinched, and so I wasn't looking out for it to be stolen. The bally things all look alike anyway. Even if it was driven straight past me, it's unlikely that I would have noticed it specifically.'

'Does that clear up the mystery of Giuseppe's missing hat and jacket?' said Felicity.

'I believe it does,' said Lady Gayle. 'The countess took the jacket and the hat to disguise herself, putting them back later when the coast was clear. Because it was siesta, she never expected Giuseppe to notice his things were gone.'

'I think that provides enough evidence for an arrest,' said Commander Ricciardi. 'We'll still need to confirm that she can drive, but all we'll need to do is contact the War Office in London.' Clasping Countess Beatrice's elbow, the commander helped her to her feet. He nodded at Constable Ferri, who produced a pair of uncomfortable-looking handcuffs.

When the countess's hands were secured, Constable Ferri escorted her from the room.

Commander Ricciardi gave the company a quick bow and followed his prisoner.

'Is it over?' The question came from Oliver Thornton. 'Am I free?'

'You are, Oliver,' said Lady Gayle. 'Unfortunately, I can't restore your fortune as easily, but I can restore your good name.'

'Perhaps I can sue Earl Harding's estate for restitution,' mused Oliver.

'I think you'll be just one person in a very long queue of people with exactly the same idea,' said Lady Gayle. 'It might be a better idea to find another way of making a living.'

'He's coming to America with me,' said Jane Blues. She leaned over and gave Oliver a peck on the cheek. 'I'm going to need a new manager.'

'What's happening with the gorilla?' said Felicity. 'Are you putting him in a zoo?'

'Cedric will be staying here at the club,' said Jane. 'He's bought me out, and with the money from that, I'm going to open a blues joint in New York. Oliver is going to help me run it.'

'I'm really happy for you both,' said Lady Gayle. 'I'm sure it will be a great success.'

She rose and glanced around at the rest of the group. No one else seemed to be keen to share what their plans were, so, feeling completely exhausted by the excitement of the day, she headed towards her bedroom.

As she reached the bottom of the stairs, Lady Gayle heard footsteps and a light cough. She sighed, knowing exactly who it was.

'You haven't asked me what my plans are.' Charles' voice was soft, but the slight quiver in his tone gave away his true feelings.

'Are you not returning to England? I'm sure we'll run into each other. Lady Ridgewell wrote to tell me that Binky is thinking of buying a racehorse.'

Charles rolled his eyes. 'Give me strength. We've just got him out of one mess, and he jumps, feet first, into the next one.'

Lady Gayle grinned. 'You may be right, but he has someone else as a part-owner. I'm sure they'll keep him straight.'

'We can only hope.' Charles reached for her hand, 'but I have other hopes too.'

His touch was cool and light. Part of Lady Gayle's instinct was to snatch her hand back, but at the same time, she didn't want to hurt him.

'I...' he began.

She shook her head and disengaged her hand. 'I'm sorry, Charles, please don't say anything. Our time has passed. We had fun before the war, but we were very young, and times have changed.'

'You have changed,' he said. 'You used to be a lot more fun. Even after the war, you were more fun than now.'

'Have I changed, or have I just grown up?' Lady Gayle swallowed, she had to say it now, or there would be more moments like this in the future. 'You haven't changed, Charles. You're still as feckless as ever you were. If ever I were to marry again, I'd need someone to share my life as it is now.' She took a deep breath. Her words had surprised her. She'd always been so adamant that there would never be anyone else. No one could replace her beloved Hugh. But perhaps there could be. 'I want someone to work with me and run the Bethencourt estate with me. Someone who loves that land as much as I do.'

'Your policeman will never do that,' snapped Charles.

Lady Gayle gazed at him, her eyes widening with surprise. 'Who on earth was thinking about Inspector Coward? I certainly wasn't.'

She closed her eyes in a slow blink as realisation suddenly hit her. Her words were clearly a shock to Charles too. 'I'm sorry, Charles—however, I think it's best if we never speak of this again.'

She turned away and hurried up the stairs to her bedroom. Bursting in, she made Alice jump. 'Alice, start packing. We're returning home just as soon as I can organise our train tickets.'

'At once, milady,' replied Alice. She flung open the doors to the armoire and lifted her ladyship's suitcase from the base.

Lady Gayle pulled out dresses and skirts, flinging them onto the bed—she'd make time to have a last breakfast with Felicity in the morning—but she really needed to get home to Bethencourt and a certain land agent.

The End

Please see below for a note on spellings used by this British author.

To my lovely readers,

A very long time ago, I was born in Britain. I love this little island and all its quirks. There are some things that I don't love, but they will never be in the Cassie Rush books.

I do use UK English spellings, punctuation, and grammar, including the "u" in colour, humour, rigour, and other words I can't think of right now. I also use an "s" where Americans tend to prefer a "z", such as cosy/cozy. In fact, my laptop just auto-corrected cozy!

I read a vast number of cosy mysteries written by American writers. I love the sarcasm, humour and I especially love the paranormal, witchy novels. It's also made me acutely aware of how the grammar differs between the two languages. It still jars when I read something like, "The dress fit perfectly" instead of, what to me is the correct form, "The dress fit**ted** perfectly", but I know it's different, not wrong.

I hope you'll forgive me for sticking with the language I've been using all my life.

Thanks,
Cassie
Suffolk, UK
October 2023

Acknowledgments

Getting a book ready for publication is a huge team effort and I'm lucky to be surrounded by such supportive friends and dedicated professionals to make my books the best they can be.

Huge thanks to my friends Nola Li Blair and Heidi Robertson who did more read throughs for me after my editor had run her blue pencil over it.

To the fabulous Molly Burton who creates the magnificent covers for the Lady Gayle Summer series, the Eastwold-by-the-Sea series and for the other series that I am currently working on; they will be out soon.

Thanks
Cassie
Suffolk 2023

ABOUT THE AUTHOR

Hi there, my name is Cassie Rush and I'm a British author of cosy mysteries set in the English country- or seaside.

I absolutely love the coastal town of Southwold which is a short drive up the coast from where I live. It's why I chose to set my popular, Eastwold by the Sea series there. Although my version of the town is entirely fictional as I like to move streets around. I hate it when an author sets a story somewhere you know well and gets details wrong, don't you?

I have been a fan of Agatha Christie all my life and I adore the other golden age authors. I especially enjoy the stories of Miss Marple, Father Brown, Brother Cadfael and Lord Peter Wimsey.

I was really lucky at school (let's not talk about how long ago that was though) to have brilliant and enthusiastic history teachers. It's given me a lifelong love of history and all the tales that the past has to offer.

Please join my newsletter here, if you would like to keep in touch, and hear news about my upcoming books and latest releases

I also write as Caroline Goldsworthy—these books are rather darker with more graphic content.

Thank you,

ALSO BY CASSIE RUSH

EASTWOLD BY THE SEA SERIES

Raising the Roof

Literary Murder

On the Stroke of Death

A Slice of Murder

LADY GAYLE SUMMER SERIES

Summers Slain

Summer Knights

Summer Secrets

Coming soon — Summer Races. The flat racing season has begun, and Lord Ridgewell has bought himself a racehorse. What could possibly go wrong?